Stories by Contemporary Writers from Shanghai

BETWEEN CONFIDANTES

This book is edited and designed by the Editorial Committee of *Cultural China* series

Text by Chen Danyan
Translation by Qiu Maoru, Yang Shuhui, Yang Yunqin
Cover Image by Quanjing
Interior Design by Xue Wenqing
Cover Design by Wang Wei

Copy Editor: Nina Train Choa
Editor: Wu Yuezhou
Editorial Director: Zhang Yicong

Senior Consultants: Sun Yong, Wu Ying, Yang Xinci
Managing Director and Publisher: Wang Youbu

ISBN: 978-1-60220-237-5

Address any comments about *Between Confidantes* to:

Better Link Press
99 Park Ave
New York, NY 10016
USA

or

Shanghai Press and Publishing Development Company
F 7 Donghu Road, Shanghai, China (200031)
Email: comments_betterlinkpress@hotmail.com

Printed in China by Shanghai Donnelley Printing Co., Ltd.

1 3 5 7 9 10 8 6 4 2

BETWEEN CONFIDANTES

Two Novellas

By Chen Danyan

Better Link Press

Foreword

This collection of books for English readers consists of short stories and novellas published by writers based in Shanghai. Apart from a few who are immigrants to Shanghai, most of them were born in the city, from the latter part of the 1940s to the 1980s. Some of them had their works published in the late 1970s and the early 1980s; some gained recognition only in the 21st century. The older among them were the focus of the "To the Mountains and Villages" campaign in their youth, and as a result, lived and worked in the villages. The difficult paths of their lives had given them unique experiences and perspectives prior to their eventual return to Shanghai. They took up creative writing for different reasons but all share a creative urge and a love for writing. By profession, some of them are college professors, some literary editors, some directors of literary institutions, some freelance writers and some professional writers. From the individual styles of the authors and the art of their writings, readers can easily detect traces of the authors' own experiences in life, their interests, as well as their aesthetic values. Most of the works in this collection are still written in the realistic style that represents, in a painstakingly fashioned fictional world, the changes of the times in urban and rural life. Having grown up in a more open era, the younger writers have been spared the hardships experienced by their predecessors, and therefore seek greater freedom in their writing. Whatever category of writers they belong to, all of them have gained their rightful places in the Chinese literary circles over the last forty years. Shanghai writers tend to favor urban narratives more than other genres of writing. Most of the works in this collection can be characterized as urban literature with Shanghai characteristics, but there are also exceptions.

Called the "Paris of the East," Shanghai was already an international metropolis in the 1920s and

30s. Being the center of China's economy, culture and literature at the time, it housed a majority of writers of importance in the history of modern Chinese literature. The list includes Lu Xun, Guo Moruo, Mao Dun and Ba Jin, who had all written and published prolifically in Shanghai. Now, with Shanghai re-emerging as a globalized metropolis, the Shanghai writers who have appeared on the literary scene in the last forty years all face new challenges and literary quests of the times. I am confident that some of the older writers will produce new masterpieces. As for the fledging new generation of writers, we naturally expect them to go far in their long writing careers ahead of them. In due course, we will also introduce those writers who did not make it into this collection.

Wang Jiren
Series Editor

Contents

Between Confidantes

1

In early summer the narrow street was dimly lit by the yellowish street lamps, which cast shadows of plane trees on the ground. The tree in front of the restaurant was decorated with many tiny Christmas lights, illuminating the restaurant's cloth streamer, which hung off a bamboo pole and swayed in the night wind.

This was one of the narrow branch streets stretching across Middle Huaihai Road. The thoroughfare was like the spine of a fish whereas the small streets looked like its little branch bones. These small, age-old streets were dimly lit because they were lined by shady plane trees. Xiaomin passed by the DDS Ballroom which had formerly been owned by a white Russian, but the days when music and singing were heard throughout the night were long gone. Nowadays, many people who returned to Shanghai after making some money working abroad settled into the old houses in those small streets, sometimes buying ground floor rooms, and opening small, stylish shops on the street side.

Xiaomin narrowed her eyes and took a sweeping glance at some of those small shops: cafés, clothing and accessory shops, small galleries and gift stores. The shops mainly sold imported goods. They were appropriately displayed and illuminated by small spotlights with black lampshades. She liked window-shopping and had a fancy for the posh goods.

She could hear music coming from an upstairs room. The classic and sentimental violin music was drifting intermittently and serenely. Loud rock 'n' roll came from behind an open window of another house. Xiaomin loosened her hair, which she had coiled for work, and let it fall on her shoulders. Viewed from behind, she looked like somebody else.

Under the protruding semi-circular door lintel at the street corner shone a tinplate-shaded lamp. The old-looking house expressed an atmosphere of colonialism typical in Old Shanghai. However, when seen more closely it was evidently renovated by modeling on the original style. But the rough wall was a little thin and the Spanish-style semi-circular window too narrow. No light could be seen from outside the house. The painted wall created a spectrum of gorgeous colors.

Xiaomin pushed the door open and walked in. There was nobody inside. Only the light on the bar counter was on. The ventilator was buzzing around her ears. The room was permeated with the mixed odor of smoke, wine and cosmetics. The smell of the cigars smoked by foreigners even filled the carpet. The boss imitated the decoration of Lan Kwai Fong in Hong Kong.

Xiaomin turned the chairs on the small round table upside down and arranged them around each table in an orderly way. She took out a wooden tray from the counter and put goblets on it. She poured water into each goblet and put a lump of red wax in the water. The ball of red wax floated in each goblet. Xiaomin laid the goblets on the tables. As she could not see the table in the dark corner clearly, the water spilled over the table. She lifted a corner of the tablecloth and wiped off the water. On the counter were the inverted wine glasses washed up the night before. Xiaomin sat down behind the counter and put a good shine on every glass. Then she hung the clean glasses on the overhead shelf.

The wall behind the counter was covered with various business cards. One card fell down. Xiaomin picked it up and found it was the business card of the general manager of a Taiwan company. Just the other day, Xiaomin had pushed a glass toward him.

"Hey, here's your one ounce. Since you're in big business, how come you only ordered one ounce?"

"Meibo, you look beautiful today. When I saw you last time, I had been wondering whether I could find really beautiful girls in Shanghai. Your beauty is beyond my imagination. You've made up my mind to invest in Shanghai. While busy with my business during the day, I'll regard it as sufficient compensation to feast my eyes on beautiful girls at night."

"Mr. Shi, you must have a string of girlfriends. Your sweet talk shows you've had a lot of practice," Xiaomin said after staring at him with a smile.

"Mr. Shi, what business are you in?"

"Did you forget the business card I gave you? I'm a jeweler."

"Imported Italian jewelry ... fascinating."

"Those jewels are covered with gold veneer and are used by fashionable girls to set off their clothing. My wife has a big box of those kinds of inexpensive jewels," he said gesticulating. "Every time she came to my shop, she picked up one jewel after another, like buying apples in a supermarket. I said to her, you're so fat that your fingers look like white turnips. I mean a fat white turnip instead of a slim carrot. If you wear a ring on your fat fingers, you will end up highlight your ugliest features."

Xiaomin rocked with laughter and leaned on the counter, saying, "Be careful! I'm afraid your wife will hunt you down here and beat you up." The man had then patted Xiaomin's hand on the counter.

Her clear memory of that meeting amused her, but she thought she would be frightened to death if she lived the rest of her life with such a talkative and cynical man. At the thought of this, she threw his business card into the dark corner.

The doorbell rang and a girl appeared in a flash. She looked around indifferently. Xiaomin recognized her; she was a university student majoring in Japanese. She recalled a comment An'an had made. An'an thought girls like this looked like women she saw in the movies.

The girl, named Linda, sat on the stool in front of the bar counter. Only now did Xiaomin notice her make-up. She had used dark brown lipstick to draw a bold line on her lips.

She worked in her spare time as a bar girl. The bosses who had returned from Japan liked girls of her type. That's why they came to the bar every day to earn extra money. Until she found a patron, she could drink at the expense of the bar. After a patron picked her up as his drinking partner, she would settle her account with the fee paid by the patron. Since she was fluent in spoken Japanese, she became a favorite of Japanese customers. Some Japanese men called her Yang Guifei, the name of a famous imperial concubine in ancient China, which they used to flatter Chinese girls. As a result, she never owed the bar for her drinks. But she always said she was short of money. Judging from her accent, she came from the north of China. In a bar like this, no bar girl talked about her private affairs or made any enquiries about others' personal matters. This had become a common practice among them. The bar girls each had a foreign name and that was all they knew each other about.

"You're the favorite of the patrons. How come you never have any money?" said Xiaomin.

"I'm fond of making merry." Linda pouted her lips and patted her purse. Her coquettish action revealed her childishness. Looking at her, Xiaomin wondered what her parents would think of if they learned they had done everything they could to send their daughter to Shanghai in pursuit of higher education and their daughter had ended up in this business, in this dazzling world.

In fact Xiaomin showed An'an that she herself was a popular girl, but at heart she did not admit she belonged to Linda's type. In her mind, they were outsiders who enjoyed their life without any long-term plan. Actually, she imagined they were losers in Shanghai. She was wiser than they were.

Xiaomin worked as a barmaid instead of a bar girl. Mainly this was because she had worked here for a much longer period than other girls. The boss was aware that she did not come here to earn her livelihood by selling her body. That's why he trusted her. Xiaomin knew very well the boss did not trust the bar girls, though he needed them to encourage customers to buy drinks. He never let them come in and stay behind the counter. The bar girls were like small fish swimming into and out of a giant shark's mouth. As for herself, she was like a tooth in the shark's mouth. In order to show her gratitude for the boss's trust, she never acted against his interests. The other reason she wasn't a bar girl was her background in nursing. As a hospital nurse, Xiaomin had soft and dexterous movements. She looked very professional when she poured drinks, never spilling a drop. The customers would feel comfortable while being served perfect drinks. And so, she got the best job at the bar.

The doorbell rang and a man came in.

"Come on in, Mister."

Xiaomin rose slightly and greeted the customer with a smile.

The man pursed his upper lip and smiled without saying anything.

"Glad to meet you," Linda greeted him in Japanese when she saw his pursed lip.

The Japanese customer climbed up the high stool

while grinning happily.

Xiaomin wiped clean a whisky glass and took down a bottle of JW Black Label Scotch from the shelf. She asked, "Do you like this?"

Before she got an answer, she quickly and smoothly poured the Scotch whisky into the glass and pushed it across the counter near his hand. She said loudly and choosing her words carefully, "This gentleman is doing business in Shanghai. He looks like the chairman of a board."

"Do you think he looks like Mr. Shi?" Linda moved to the high stool next to the Japanese man and addressed Xiaomin while glancing at the man.

Xiaomin moved her head closer to have a good look at the puzzled Japanese man, saying, "Do you mean that Taiwanese bumpkin?"

"Look at his nose. Do they look alike? According to the book on physiognomy, people with that kind of nose have good luck in money matters."

Xiaomin fixed her eyes on his clean red nose in the lamplight, saying, "Really? Then I must treat the Taiwanese man better next time he comes."

She pointed to the Japanese man and said with a

smile, "We said you're beautiful."

"Shanghai ladies, the young ones, are beautiful," he said.

Xiaomin glanced at Linda, saying, "Another Japanese lecher! Ever since they started their aggression against the Chinese people, they have been lecherous."

"She said if you like us, you should drink more and have fun," Linda said to him in Japanese.

Xiaomin and Linda nodded their heads politely and found it amusing.

2

When she pushed the door open, Xiaomin found the newly renovated room was decorated with pink wallpaper. Its gaily-colored patterns were dazzling in the light of a few naked bulbs. The lampshades were not up yet.

Xiaomin and the thin tall man stood side by side at the doorstep. He was her friend An'an's husband. His lean face and fair complexion displayed a calculating yet indifferent look which was typical of the men of southern cities. He stood against the newly painted white door frame with his arms around his shoulders.

"It looks fabulous," said Xiaomin.

"The wallpaper was imported from England. No kidding. You know how expensive it is!" He pointed his finger in all directions, saying, "The windows were replaced with white ones. An'an drew her inspiration from American images. She said in America doors and windows were all painted white. I had to use all my connections to find this floor paint. It's made in Hong Kong."

"Little Chen, I know you're wealthy," Xiaomin cast a glance at him and said with a smile.

"This renovation cost me a lot. I've run out of money," he said. "I don't earn as easily as you girls working at a café. You need only flash your customer a sweet smile, and he will give you his money willingly. Am I right?"

"I don't want to borrow money from you."

"As soon as you put in a request, I'll lend all my savings to you."

Little Chen fixed the lamp over the basin in

the white bathroom. When he turned on the light, the room was pink. Xiaomin uttered a sound of amazement. Little Chen said, "What do you think of it? Is it sexy?"

They took a sweeping glance at the bathroom. The white ceramic fixtures became pink in the light and the new taps were shining brightly.

Xiaomin found Little Chen's face overbearing and aggressive in the pink light. She imagined that An'an must have found herself in similar circumstances. His face often looked graceful, but sometimes it would suddenly take on the aggressive expression of a beast. She thought this expression might make a woman sense the thrill of being chased. Women like to be chased. Of course they like to be chased by a man they have taken a fancy to. But the choice is made by the woman before the start of the chase.

When Little Chen started to court An'an, Xiaomin had felt a little distressed. At that time An'an knew that Little Chen was a really good candidate. It so happened that he had been hospitalized for an appendectomy. Otherwise An'an would not have gotten to know this promising young man. When

An'an eventually got married, Xiaomin suddenly felt she herself was already an old maid. It made her think that she too ought to manage to get married like An'an, and sleep on a fashionable king-size bed.

With the help of the light she fixed her eyes on Little Chen. She recalled a dream she had. In her dream she had her own family; a man was walking to and fro in an ordinary room. This man was her husband. She walked toward him with something in her hand. All of a sudden, she found it was Little Chen. In her dream, she was surprised and had asked herself: Isn't he An'an's husband? How did he become her husband? Xiaomin's interpretation of this dream was that she was anxious to get married.

In the pink light everything seemed out of focus and everything felt dream-like.

Little Chen fixed his eyes on her. She found it strange and tried to avoid his direct gaze. She faltered and their eyes locked together in the small pink room.

"What do you think of it?" asked Little Chen.

"Not bad."

Later, as they walked through a furnishing shop,

Xiaomin remembered the dream again. Xiaomin and Little Chen moved slowly toward an area where a variety of curtains were displayed. They felt the different materials.

Xiaomin pulled out a sample curtain with a cheerful, colored pattern, saying, "Does An'an like this?"

They moved a few steps away and looked at the sample curtain from a distance.

The salesgirl came over, saying, "You have a keen eye for works of art. This type of curtain was recently imported and is on sale only in our shop. It is most suitable for the decoration of a new room. If you buy more, I can offer you 10% off."

Xiaomin kept silent and glanced at Little Chen.

Little Chen had a white linen jacket on and its broad padded shoulder touched Xiaomin's shoulder while they stood side by side. Xiaomin did not say anything or move away. Standing motionlessly against Little Chen's shoulder, Xiaomin was examining the beautiful cloth.

"This pattern looks even more fantastic in the lamplight. It will emit golden rays," continued the salesgirl.

Xiaomin asked, "Does the golden color match the color of the wallpaper?"

Little Chen patted his jacket, saying, "Just say the word and I'll pay for it. It's up to you to decide."

Xiaomin intended to say: "It's not my home. How can I have the final say?" But when she cast a glance at the attentive salesgirl, she knew the salesgirl looked upon her as the decision maker. As soon as she gave an approving nod, her "husband" would pay for it. The salesgirl was hoping to clinch a big deal. Xiaomin leant lightly against the padded shoulder of Little Chen's jacket.

"The wallpaper of our room is pink," Xiaomin said to the salesgirl.

"We have a silvery pattern which would match pink perfectly." The salesgirl showed another pattern to Xiaomin and Little Chen.

Xiaomin declared, "This pattern is much better." She turned her head and looked at Little Chen, saying, "What do you think of it?"

The salesgirl said, "This lady has a keen eye. Her taste is excellent. To be frank, this pattern is really fantastic. I know you'd rather spend money on the best goods. Curtains are durable consumer goods and it's a once-only buy."

Little Chen said, "OK, I'll take it."

Xiaomin and Little Chen then raised their heads and looked at a variety of brightly lit lamps.

Xiaomin liked a glass chandelier with a complex pattern and indicated this to Little Chen by patting him on the shoulder.

Little Chen asked the salesgirl to bring one to them. They saw the price tag: "2,200 yuan." Little Chen cast a glance at Xiaomin and carefully examined the chandelier with his hands.

"I like this kind of chandelier most because it gives the room an air of elegance," said Xiaomin.

"The chandeliers sold at this shop are priced 50% higher than those at other shops," said Little Chen.

"Not exactly," said the salesgirl who was still keeping them company.

Little Chen said with a grin, "I know better than you as I myself am in the lighting business. If it is made in Wenzhou, the price is reasonable."

Xiaomin said to the salesgirl, "In this respect I advise you not to argue with him because that's his line of work."

The salesgirl nodded her head and said in a calm and collected manner, "I'm not arguing with this gentleman. Since this gentleman is in this business, he's certainly more professional. I only meant to say, the chandelier this lady likes is in great demand at our shop. If newly-weds can afford this kind of chandelier, the gentleman is certainly a good businessman. It's important to add an impressive air to your house. As ours is a big shop, the quality of our goods is guaranteed. The chandelier will be hanging over your heads, so its quality is very important. You will feel comfortable and safe, even though it's a little expensive."

Little Chen was amused by her glib tongue and said, "You're so eloquent. You're wasting your talent on selling lamps here."

Xiaomin said, "Why don't you employ her as a PR lady in your company?"

The salesgirl cracked a smile and held the chandelier carefully in her hands. She said, "That's more than I could wish for."

Little Chen gesticulated to the salesgirl and asked

her to pack it up. Then he paid the money. Xiaomin stood by his side, smiling radiantly. Her eyes scanned the whole shop to see whether there was anything else worth buying. She walked across the brilliantly lit marble floor with light and quick steps. She examined a bronze-colored standing lamp by moving around it. Modeled after an antique, the lamp was covered with a frosted glass lampshade, which looked like a bowler hat Sun Yat-sen used to wear. The lampshade was painted with red flowers and a golden edge.

She said merrily and loudly, "Come here! This lamp could be placed behind the sofa. When I was a child, there was a standing lamp like this in Grandma's house. It looked so splendid." She clasped her hands in front of her chest and said with emotion, "Nowadays there are so many attractive things." She recalled the days when she lived at her grandparents' house. Grandpa had worked as a broker before liberation. After China was liberated in 1949, he took special care of the family property. He kept the family belongings ranging from a wardrobe to a standing floor lamp in good condition so that he could imagine that he was still leading a former, grander life behind closed doors. Grandma never allowed the children to turn on the floor lamp for fear that they might pull too hard and break the lamp's string made of tiny steel beads. Grandma used to say, "This lamp was imported from America. Where can I find a matching lamp string if you break it?"

In her parents' house all the furniture was bought during the Cultural Revolution. Not a single piece was refined, beautiful or elegant. In Xiaomin's mind, her parents' house was not a home at all. Only her grandparents' house could be regarded as a home. She was influenced by her grandmother in other ways too. She applied for admission to a nurses' school after her graduation from high school. Her grandmother had been an experienced nurse and had inspired her choice of career. After she stopped working she had always dressed herself fashionably and taken care to keep herself fit. During her childhood, Xiaomin had been fascinated by Grandma's gentle and capable temperament.

The big drawer in Grandma's house was full of well preserved old articles which were the memories Grandma cherished of her former, nicer days.

Xiaomin liked to look at the old photos of Grandma. To Xiaomin, even the nurse's uniform Grandma wore in the photos looked gorgeous.

Before liberation, Grandma served as a nurse at the first-class ward. She was born into an ordinary family. However, when she worked at the first-class ward, she had the opportunity to get acquainted with Grandpa. At that time, Grandpa had been a promising young broker who had been successful in several major deals. When he contracted appendicitis and suffered from abdominal angina, he managed to register into the first-class ward. Both an optimist and a hedonist, the young patient fell in love with the young nurse. And so Grandma was married into a good family. Grandma used to joke: if nothing had happened in 1949, your grandpa would have brouhgt me an even better life. During those days she stayed at home as a full-time housewife. Only after liberation did she go back to the hospital and work as a nurse again.

When she was a child, Xiaomin assumed that being a nurse was a direct road to marrying a man with a distinguished family background and to leading a comfortable life. She too could have a bronze standing floor lamp made in America in her own house. She would put the lamp behind the sofa and the yellowish lamplight would fall in a pool on the floor.

Xiaomin clasped Little Chen's hand and looked at the lamp, saying, "In the evening it will be a treat to read a novel while sitting on the sofa by the light of the lamp."

She sincerely hoped that he would buy the lamp and let her place it behind the sofa in the living room. She didn't remember seeing the sofa during her last visit. But she was sure that An'an had told her they had bought a new sofa.

She cast a glance at Little Chen. He was examining the lamp carefully with his narrow eyes. She put her arm into the crook of his arm and pushed him gently. He cast a glance at her. In the lamplight her cheeks were rosy with excitement. She had an appealing look in her eyes. He saw the reflection of various shades of brilliant light in her brown eyes.

The salesgirl brought them the packed-up chandelier and said to Little Chen, "Your wife has a keen eye. This antique-model floor lamp is in our new stock."

"Since we buy so much at your shop, you ought to give us a discount," said Xiaomin.

When Little Chen took out the money from the inner pocket of his jacket and paid for the lamp, Xiaomin's face slightly reddened. She held his arm in hers and shouted smilingly, "Hurrah, what a terrific guy you are!" They carried all their purchases and went to the café on the top floor of the department store.

The café in this deluxe department store was an ideal place for shoppers to take a break. The brightly-lit café with melodious background music sold ice cream which was flown in from America. The waitresses wore Japanese-style green-striped aprons, and were serving customers with light steps. The shoppers put their purchases proudly on the nearby chairs. Some people were carefully stirring the coffee in their cups; others were eating ice cream one small bite at a time, as if they were savoring the precious food. Two fashionable young women were smoking by the window. The nails of their slender fingers were painted red. They fastened their cold eyes on Xiaomin and Little Chen first, and then on the shop names printed on the plastic bags they were carrying.

While turning around, Xiaomin deliberately rearranged the plastic bags she was carrying and placed the bag of the most expensive shop outward in a calm and collected manner. Then she lifted her chin slightly and put on an air of indifference. This was a common trick Shanghai ladies used while walking on the streets. They liked to display their most splendid side to passers-by. They did not operate with the heavy hand of an overnight millionaire, but instead casually waited for others to discover their wealth.

To all appearances, the natives of Shanghai seem to be always calculating and sorting things out. Outsiders might think they were too shrewd. As a matter of fact, Shanghai ladies' cool calculations are not at the expense of others. What they are really concerned about is saving "face" in order not to look bad.

Little Chen pointed to the corner table. The receptionist ushered them to the table.

They sat down at the table. Xiaomin glanced around and said, "At last there's a place in Shanghai where we can have a rest."

Little Chen stared at Xiaomin, saying, "Do you know what was in my mind when you followed me into the café?"

Xiaomin shrugged her shoulders.

"I thought that you are a presentable companion."

Xiaomin said, "I'm flattered. How honey-lipped you are!"

Xiaomin pointed at the candle in the center of the table. Little Chen took out a cigarette lighter and lit the candle. The lit red candle illuminated their eyes. As the light shone up on their faces from below, their appearance seemed to change. They fastened their eyes on each other across the table, which was decorated with two multi-colored glass ice cream bowls and a delicate fresh rose.

Once back at the apartment, the floor-length curtains with gaily-colored patterns and silver stripes looked splendid in the light. Little Chen walked back and forth between the room and the hallway, moving everything in the boxes into the room. He opened a cardboard box containing books, metallic paintings and picture frames. He moved the box into the room and took out its contents one by one. There was an enlarged picture of two chubby girls in the intern nurse's uniform standing under a cedar. They cuddled together and smiled broadly. They were An'an and Xiaomin studying at the nurses' school.

The next framed picture showed An'an in a white wedding dress holding a bunch of red roses. Faced with a dozen guests standing around the big dining table and raising their glasses of wine, An'an was turning to Xiaomin for help. An'an's beauty was beyond description. Xiaomin was wearing a pink sleeveless *qipao* and was holding out her snow-white arm to stop the wine-filled glass from reaching An'an's mouth. She raised her glass of wine with the other arm and intended to drink on behalf of An'an.

Little Chen lifted his head and glanced at Xiaomin who was standing on the table. The close-fitting thin black dress enveloped her mature body. She was no longer a fat teenage girl. Nor was she as conventional as she had been when she served as a bridesmaid. Viewed from behind, she seemed to be covered with a layer of dark skin, which was warm and inviting reminding him of something warm in winter.

He pushed the picture frames into the back of the wardrobe. He closed the door of the wardrobe and leant against it watching Xiaomin. Clad in the black blouse and pants she wore at the bar, Xiaomin stood on the table in front of the window and tried to fix the curtains. She raised her arms high and the movement of her clothing made her look even more charming. He thought that since Xiaomin mingled all day long with men who were richer and more brazen than he himself was, she must be more familiar with amorous feelings than his own wife.

Whenever he heard a story about a bar girl, he would imagine that everything was happening to Xiaomin.

He was always cautious and discreet. Without a distinguished family background, he had worked very hard and was promoted gradually from a Youth League cadre to the most fashionable and profitable post in the company—Deputy Director of the Trade Department.

He discovered that many of his colleagues were enticed by their clients into karaoke clubs and ended up losing their standing and reputations, which was why he acted very cautiously and never visited such places. However, every time he passed by one of them, he would say to himself, I'll come here some day and intoxicate myself. In his mind, he thought he wouldn't be a real man if he hadn't spent time in bars and been waited upon by women working in those places. But he was a highly motivated man and would not put himself in danger simply to satisfy fleeting desires. Nevertheless, he was a man, and like all the other men, he had a natural curiosity and desire about dissolute women and their sex life. Men may not love bad women, but they certainly want to have a taste of them. In their minds, they can't be heroes until they conquer those women.

Sometimes while chatting with An'an in their spare time, he asked her about Xiaomin's life at the bar. An'an told him that Xiaomin worked there for the sole purpose of hunting for an ideal rich husband. She never sold her body. He would grin cheekily and said, "To hunt for a good husband, she should acquire good skills in bed so as to raise her selling price." Exasperated by his remarks, An'an would throw pillows at him. These dramatic moments often served as foreplay for their lovemaking.

Xiaomin focused her attention on the task of

hanging the curtains on the rod so that she could put the floor lamp in place.

In her mind's eye, Grandma's living room had a narrow steel French window, a sofa beside the window and a standing lamp behind the sofa. In the gentle light that she imagined emitted from behind, you could put an English novel on the sofa and a cup of milky coffee on the coffee table and as soon as you caught sight of its color, you could imagine its delicious taste.

As soon as she had hung the curtains, Xiaomin placed the standing lamp in just the right spot.

The lamp was fascinating. The light emitted by the frosted glass was so soft that she could not see the wrinkles on the back of her hand. Xiaomin lay down on the sofa with her face upward as if her body was melting. She had never decorated a house herself. She had never known she had such fiery passion in her heart. She could only sense the ringing in her ears and all of a sudden felt like she was being plunged into an abyss.

Right there and then she saw Little Chen approaching. In the shadows of the lamplight she could not see his face clearly. He seemed to her like a strange lump, giving out heat and belching black smoke.

She heard herself swallow her saliva noisily.

Little Chen came over and embraced her tightly. Under the weight of two people, the sofa heaved a long sigh. The fresh smell of the new leather was emanating from the depth of the sofa. With an enquiring smile on her face, Xiaomin stared at Little Chen and then clasped his neck in her arms.

3

The day dawned bright and sunny.

Sunlight filtered through the crevice of the brightly colored curtains. The chandelier which Xiaomin had chosen the day before was hanging from the center of the ceiling. Its branching glass bulbs looked sparkly in the ray of sunshine.

The brand-new furniture in the room created a strange and warm atmosphere reminiscent of a wedding chamber.

On the floor between the door and the king-size bed near the window were scattered black pantyhose, a pair of white panties, a flower-patterned skirt, an undershirt and a pair of blue briefs.

On the king size bed Xiaomin and Little Chen rested their heads together on the same pillow. Xiaomin was leaning forward when she was pulled back by Little Chen, still with his eyes closed. Xiaomin giggled. Xiaomin bent forward again and saw her own face clearly. Her rosy cheeks and enchanting look made her tender, beautiful and charming she thought. She sat on the edge of the bed and inhaled deeply. Her eyes scanned the sunlight-blocked room.

"Are you crazy? What a mess on the floor!" Xiaomin was in a cheerful mood, nonetheless complaining.

"Yesterday you said you liked the way it was," said Little Chen.

"Don't talk nonsense," Xiaomin yelled while a flush of embarrassment rose to her cheeks. "You drank too much at the restaurant and went out of your mind." Almost at the same time she turned round and threw herself on Little Chen. She pulled his ear and started to bite it. Little Chen pulled her back and embraced her again in his arms. Xiaomin said, "It's time to go to work. If I'm late every day, I'll be fired." Xiaomin struggled out of Little Chen's embrace. She picked up her clothes off the floor and covered her naked body. She saw Little Chen leaning against the pillow and looked her up and down with a mischievous smile.

"Don't look at me. I'm putting on my clothes."

"Don't forget you're a bar girl. I don't think you are wearing trendy enough clothes," said Little Chen.

Xiaomin loosened her grip on her clothes. She looked around and went to a line of mirrored wardrobes. She opened one wardrobe and took out a green dress. She let go of the clothes in her hand in a casual manner and they fell down slowly on the floor. Bathed in the pink light coming from the crevice of the curtains, the naked woman in the mirror brimmed with the warm feelings of sexual satisfaction.

"You were very responsive. How do they describe this in books, oh yes, a man and a woman are caught in a burning passion just like dry wood placed near a raging fire," Little Chen said behind her.

Xiaomin was smiling shyly at Little Chen in the mirror. She carefully lifted her feet and pulled on some new pantyhose.

He said, "Black suits you best. I like a woman wearing black pantyhose. Your ankles look nice."

Xiaomin began to put on her clothes.

He said, "Don't forget to bring my beeper with you. As soon as I get the porn videotape, I'll call you. To be frank, there's nothing extraordinary. If we tape our own lovemaking, our performance will be even better than theirs."

Xiaomin rushed all the way to work. The long green hallway of the hospital shone brightly from the sunlight which filtered through the lattice windows. A group of probationers from the nurses' school were walking in the hallway. Xiaomin tied up her hair in the blue nurse's cap and tightened the waist so as to let the lower hem of the white gown spread out like a skirt. She walked in a serious and graceful manner.

At the end of the hallway Xiaomin came to a sudden halt and said, "In the afternoon what's the duty of a nurse at the ward?"

"Dispense medication," said a girl with rosy cheeks.

"What should a nurse pay attention to when

she dispenses medication?" asked Xiaomin. She stopped before she completed her question. She felt something and touched her breast pocket instantly. There was a faint flush on her face. She put down her hand immediately and continued to ask, "Who can tell us about the points to pay attention to when dispensing medication?"

"Check the bed number and the patient's name against the doctor's treatment order," the previous girl answered.

"What else?" said Xiaomin.

"And—" the student nurse hesitated.

"You should check the name of the medicine against the doctor's treatment order," Xiaomin said hurriedly. "Next time you should give a quicker answer. It's important for a nurse to act quickly."

She felt her breast pocket vibrating again. She crossed her arms on her breast and pointed her chin to the students, saying, "As for today, you can study by yourselves or ask your supervisors to see whether they give you any assignments."

She walked in quick steps toward her office which stood in the middle of the hallway. She turned her head and said to them, "I want to remind you, you should never run in the hospital because it will make the patients feel nervous. Even if something requiring your urgent attention happens, you must remain calm and collected. You can walk, of course in quick steps."

The probationers who stood at the end of the hallway watched Xiaomin walking quickly and then, finally, running into her office.

They could not help laughing. One girl said to others, "What about setting an example with one's own conduct, do we do that?"

The other girls shook their heads and said in unison, "No, we don't."

The girl with rosy cheeks raised her hands to squeeze her fat face and made it look like Xiaomin's thin face. She said in a muffled voice, "You should never run in the hospital. Even if something urgent happens, you must remain calm and collected."

They all had a great laugh about it. The young girls' laughter filled the hospital's hallway and its tinkling sound resounded like broken glass.

Xiaomin, who had run into the office, poked her head out of the door. All the probationers lapsed into a sudden silence. Xiaomin said to the head nurse who was checking the medicine cabinet, "I have to write a report in my office. I'll leave the student nurses here to get familiar with their working environment."

Xiaomin rushed down the stairs and found a quiet place. She took out the beeper from her breast pocket. When she had a look at it, she cracked a smile. Then she hurried down the stairs again.

When she saw a colleague in a white gown, she said, "I forgot to write the report required by the administrative office. I'm sure they will give me a dressing-down."

"Why didn't you take the elevator?"

"I was too impatient to wait."

Xiaomin held the handrail, turned at the stairwell and disappeared.

"Take care!" her colleague shouted.

"If I tumble down and kill myself, do remember to attend my memorial meeting." Xiaomin's merry laughter came from a distance. Xiaomin bumped against people on her way. She rushed forward and got on the bus the minute before the door was closed. She found a high seat on the wheel and sat down clasping her drawn-up knees. She took out Little Chen's beeper and looked at it again. Xiaomin hurried up the stairs. The hallway of the new dormitory was tainted with cement spots, grey dust and the cardboard boxes which the new tenants used to dispose of the rubbish as they moved in. Xiaomin skirted the boxes and saw the big tree outside the window. Bathed in the sunshine of early summer, the green leaves of the tree remained absolutely still. Xiaomin held out her hand as if she wanted to stroke them. Her hand gleamed in the sunlight.

One household was still putting up interior decorations. When Xiaomin passed by, the electric drill suddenly started to trill noisily. Through the open door, Xiaomin saw a woman standing on the table trying to hang up a curtain. It was a brightly colored curtain. With the curtain blown up by the wind, the flowing flower patterns filled Xiaomin's eyes.

Her ears were almost deafened by the penetrating sound of the electric drill as if the flowers and sunshine were yelling at her. The gaily-colored cloth was swaying gently in the sunlight and in the early summer breeze. The background noise was terrible. Xiaomin rushed up the stairs. As she inserted the key in the lock the door opened from the inside. Little Chen pulled her in and embraced her closely.

There was a thin and high cedar at the entrance of the hospital. It was not green. A blackboard stood against the trunk of the cedar. On the blackboard there was a bunch of flowers drawn with colored chalk and underneath a slogan read: "The hospital welcomes the medical team coming back home from the afflicted area!"

Xiaomin walked into the hospital at a quick pace. She felt flustered. With dark rings round her eyes, she looked slack and tired. She was absent-minded. She walked past the blackboard. Then she suddenly realized what she had seen and halted her steps. She read the slogan on the blackboard: "The hospital welcomes the medical team coming back home from the afflicted area!" She had suddenly been struck by an awareness of An'an.

The probationers of the nurses' school came out of the dormitory in twos and threes. They were going to the inpatients' building. Some girls imitated Xiaomin and tightened the waist of their white uniforms so as to emphasize their figures. When they passed by Xiaomin, they greeted her in a polite way. Their greeting awakened Xiaomin, who was focusing her eyes on the blackboard.

Xiaomin turned her head and glanced at them. As she suddenly turned in the direction of the sun, the sunlight streamed directly in her eyes. She shaded her face with her hand. The silvery butterfly-shaped ring on her finger glittered in the sunlight. She pointed to the girl in the middle, saying, "Who told you to let your hair out of the nurse's cap?"

She glanced at the other girls, saying, "How did you pass your nursing course? Don't you know hair carries pathogenic bacteria? You should put your hair entirely in your nurse's cap. This is your graduation field work. Your behavior is reprehensible!"

4

Xiaomin was eating a hot dog when she climbed up the stairs. Just like eating an ear of corn, she ate the outer roll first and then the inner sausage. She bought the hot dog at an American fast-food restaurant which had recently opened on the Bund. According to its advertisements, all the ingredients and the recipe were authentically American. It tasted quite different from other hot dogs.

She came to the door and opened it. The curtain was still drawn. The room permeated with a rancid and sweet smell from the nights of revelry. The quilt was rolled up on the big bed. It looked as if somebody were sleeping there. Xiaomin was so shocked that she almost choked on the food she was chewing. Only after she gazed fixedly at the bed did she feel relieved.

She got into the bathroom and turned on the light in front of the mirror. She took a glass and filled it up with the water from the filter. While drinking the water, she stared at herself in the mirror. In the pink light of the lamp, her face was obscured. She wiped her eyes clean, but she could not get rid of the dark rings round her eyes. She picked up a small bottle of medicine near the toothpaste. That was the contraceptive pill she took every day. She shook the bottle in front of the lamp and the sound told her that only a few pills were left. She held the bottle tightly in one hand and emptied the water from the glass and took the glass with her in the other hand.

She went into the room and opened the wardrobe. She took out a big plastic bag which she and Little Chen had used when they shopped for the curtains. She put the bottle and the glass in the plastic bag. She turned about and went to the bathroom again.

She pulled down the yellow towel from the towel rail. Her eyes scanned everywhere in the bathroom. She pulled back the half closed shower curtain and bent down to examine the bathtub closely. She picked up a long hair of hers, threw it into the toilet bowl and flushed it down. Then, she turned on the tap. She took a sponge and a bottle of multi-surface cleanser. She started to clean the bathtub thoroughly. She picked up all her stray hairs and threw them into the toilet bowl.

She drew apart the curtains and pushed open the door leading to the balcony. She moved the bedclothes to the balcony so that they could be aired in the sunshine. She clutched one end of the sheet and shook all the possible traces of herself off the sheet. She hung the sheet out on a bamboo pole and carefully checked every single inch of it. Something caught her attention and she pinched the spot. She pulled down the sheet from the bamboo pole and carried it to the bathroom. She turned on the tap. The gurgling sound of water could be heard in the hallway.

She climbed onto the uncovered mattress and checked it carefully. She found a broken hairclip of hers and crawled over to the window. She lifted up the curtain and threw the hairclip out of the window. She felt something on the curtain. She touched it with her finger and put the finger under her nose. She smelled something. She removed the curtain from the rod and carried it to the bathtub. The new curtain was submerged in the water with a soft sigh. Its color was becoming darker. She stirred the curtain and sheet with her hands and they gave off a moist and fresh smell. When she moved the sheet and tried to locate traces of herself, her finger got stuck by something and could not get free. She struggled to get free. She struggled hard with it. Finally she freed her finger from the cloth. The cloth had been hooked to the wing of her butterfly-shaped ring. She took off her ring and put it on the washbasin stand. She was intent on her washing. The breast and knees of her clothes were completely wet and her wet hair was hanging down on her face. She looked like a housewife engaged in a really thorough spring cleaning. She opened the wardrobe and removed all her clothing from the hangers, then the black panties, stockings and leotards. She put all of them into a big plastic bag.

A few picture frames caught her attention. Behind the glass she and An'an were smiling in the bright sunlight which poured through the now curtain-less window. The picture reminded Xiaomin of the days when she and An'an were still going through puberty. They looked fat and a little stupid. They became bosom buddies when they were studying together at the nurses' school. They shared a bunk bed. Xiaomin still remembered the first time she met An'an. Xiaomin was the first one to come to the dorm. After she had made up her bed, she sat on the bed and watched the late arrivals. She did not know why the girls played pampered children in the presence of their future classmates. Xiaomin despised them at heart while she fixed her eyes on them.

All of a sudden she caught sight of An'an. The chubby An'an was looking at her cousin—a university student—setting up the mosquito net for her. With her beautiful big eyes, An'an looked like an innocent lamb. Clad in a clean checked shirt, her cousin acted like a refined gentleman. She could smell the freshness of his hair.

Sometimes, you can judge a person's family background from the behavior of his friends or family members. Their behavior is more revealing than one's own. There and then Xiaomin became well disposed toward An'an. In her mind, An'an was a secure and endearing girl with a respectable social status.

Gradually they became confidantes to each other. Like best friends living at a boarding school, they went to the dining hall, to classrooms and to the boiling water stand together. In their relationship Xiaomin was domineering, active and protective whereas An'an was low-profile, soft and quiet.

Holding the picture frame in her hands, she walked to and fro in the room trying to find a suitable place to hang the frame. On the balcony outside the open door behind her, the brightly colored curtain was drying as it flapped in the wind and sunlight.

She picked up a white sock of hers from the sofa.

On the coffee table there were a couple of Pearl tea bags. She drank this brand of tea in the morning and in the evening. She crumpled the empty bags into a ball and threw them out of the window.

Finally, she decided to put up the picture frame on a small piece of unoccupied wall behind the sofa. If the lamp was turned on, the yellowish light would fall on the picture. It would create a warm family atmosphere.

All of a sudden, the electric drill was roaring again from downstairs. In order to penetrate a hard surface, the drill worked harder and the sound of the drill was grating. In another picture of Little Chen's wedding banquet, An'an and Xiaomin worked together to cope with the teasing toasters. With the ear-piercing noise coming from downstairs, Xiaomin continued to stare at the pictures on the wall.

As soon as they had graduated from the nurses' school, An'an had married Little Chen. After her first encounter with Little Chen at the ward, An'an told Xiaomin about it at lunchtime in the dining hall. She said a young man had been hospitalized at the ward she was in charge of. An'an's eyes had shone in the dimly lit dining hall. Xiaomin noticed her facial expression and pointed at her with her chopsticks, saying, "I know you like him. When you talk about him, your face flushes."

Xiaomin remembered that An'an did not answer and simply hit her on the arm. From then on, in order to show her graceful figure, An'an never wore a second sweater—even in the depth of winter. After Little Chen could move around in the ward, An'an deliberately left her keys in the nurses' station and asked Little Chen if he could open the door for her. In this way tiny An'an could raise her face to display her best expression—her endearing expression. An'an played many tricks of this kind without betraying any emotion. However, she never cracked jokes or prolonged her stay at his ward. As Little Chen became increasingly attracted to her, she would disappear more frequently.

Xiaomin was aware that An'an had given Little Chen her home address while she was performing her routine duty at the ward. A ward is a mini-society. Little Chen's ward mates noticed their unusual relationship and made fun of them. They shared the opinion that Little Chen was poisoning the youngster's mind by paying assiduous court to An'an.

At the time, Rule No. 1 for guiding trainee nurses provided that they should not have an affair with any patient. Those who violated this rule were severely punished. However, so far as An'an was concerned, nobody blamed her for her loose morals. People always thought that Little Chen was of the sentimental type. As a result, An'an found her Mr. Right and they had a joyful wedding.

Xiaomin looked at An'an's smile in the picture. An'an really rode the high tide of luck and people didn't have the heart to criticize her endearing personality.

Xiaomin went to the telephone. She called Little Chen to tell him that An'an would be back. Little Chen uttered a sound of acknowledgment and said nothing more.

Xiaomin said, "Maybe it's not convenient for you to talk. Just listen to me. I want to tell you we've lived a happy life in the past few days. But I don't want to hurt An'an's feelings, nor do I want to disrupt your family life."

"I know, I know," Little Chen said hurriedly. Little Chen's hurried reply after a short silence made

Xiaomin realize he was in a dilemma as to how to end their affair in private. In a sense she came to his rescue by taking the initiative. She knew that he saw eye to eye with her. However, as a woman, she felt a little unhappy. She was aware that she had no right to feel unhappy. But she could not imagine that he would not feel nostalgic for these romantic days. That's why she said in a cold tone, "It would be best for me to disappear completely from your life. I've sorted out everything and done the necessary laundry. Let's part from each other peacefully."

Little Chen uttered another louder, more surprised sound of acknowledgment.

Xiaomin said, "Please rest assured that nobody will know anything about this if you keep silent. I will keep silent. In my mind, nothing has occurred between us. We only went together to buy the curtains for An'an. It's you who bought all these lamps and they had nothing to do with me."

Little Chen said suddenly, "Hold on please. I'll check the latest price. We have a uniform price list. I'll call you after I check the price."

Xiaomin hung up her phone. She knew Little

Chen was going to use another phone. There must be somebody in his office. Xiaomin recalled the sound she had just heard on the phone. When he was nervous, his voice would change so much that it sounded strange to her. For the first time Xiaomin despised Little Chen. She had not paid enough attention to her best friend's husband before. Right now she held the coffee table on which the telephone was placed and said to herself, she would never marry a man who was not bold enough to make a phone call.

The phone was ringing.

Little Chen was at a loss for words. Finally he said, "I've borrowed a new videotape."

Xiaomin said, "You can play it for An'an." All of a sudden, she found her remark was too obscene. She said, "OK, that's all for us."

He said, "We don't need to make a clean break with each other as if we're strangers."

"We'd better make a clean break with each other. We each have our own life to live. Why should we have a surreptitious relationship?" Xiaomin said loudly and clearly.

"OK," Little Chen agreed.

"Bye-bye!" said Xiaomin.

"Bye-bye!" said Little Chen.

The bar was filled with cigarette smoke and high stools in front of the bar were fully occupied. Accompanied by the background music of a rock' n' roll song in English, Linda was swaying her body while sitting on a high stool. Xiaomin cast a glance at Linda. Her patron looked like a gentleman. She was giving him her attention in her most scholarly manner. Through the white smoke, her patron stared at her with a smile.

Xiaomin thought about Linda's skill. All the patrons liked her whether they came here looking for a whore or a chatting partner. She was so fluent in Japanese that she might marry a foreigner if she wished. It was said that foreigners who work in China feel very lonely, especially at night. Her future husband might even be a promising politician. But should the foreign press search thoroughly through the history of his a future wife, such a marriage would likely become a big scandal.

Xiaomin thought, it doesn't matter. Even if they get divorced, she can get half of his wealth. Then she will become a rich woman and it'll be easy for her to find her Mr. Right.

Another man came over and sat down on a high stool. Xiaomin greeted him with a smile and found it was none other than Mr. Shi from Taiwan. With a smile, Xiaomin poured a glass of wine for him and put a white paper napkin under the glass. She pushed the glass to Mr. Shi.

"Why don't you wear a ring on such a slender finger of yours, Miss?"

Xiaomin subconsciously bent her thumb to touch her ring-free middle finger. Her face darkened instantly. I've lost my ring, but where?

She cast a glance at Mr. Shi and said, "As I don't have any pretty rings, I'm waiting for your present, Mr. Shi."

"No problem. No problem. You can come to my shop and have a look."

"I'm afraid I don't have the same happy lot as your wife."

As soon as she uttered this remark, Xiaomin was aware that she had made a slip of the tongue. She kept silent and made a feint of looking at his glass. She added an ice cube to his glass. In the meantime she cast a glance at him.

The man was smiling at her without saying anything.

Xiaomin blushed crimson and cast another glance at him. He was still smiling and staring at her without saying anything. It was like an adult watching a child bragging. A flush of embarrassment rose to her cheeks and she came near to tears. In spite of her embarrassment, she fixed her eyes on him, saying, "Why are you looking at me like this? Your look is making me feel creeped out."

Linda knuckled the counter, saying, "Open a bottle of XO and give me two glasses."

"What kind of patron have you got?" asked Xiaomin.

"A Japanese man." Linda gave him a sidelong glance. "He came here to investigate the investment environment. To my surprise, he doesn't know that we also sell imported wine here. He may be mistaking China for Korea. What a laughing stock he has turned himself into! That's why I recommended a bottle of XO."

"You have a lot of fun," Xiaomin said while she turned around to fetch the wine and glasses. She picked up small plate of peanuts as well.

"I think you have a lot of fun" Linda continued, "You were both smiling broadly. Mr. Shi seems to have finally found the person he was waiting for. In recent days he has made enquiries about you every time he comes. Where's the barmaid I met the other day? He gave us the impression that the other girls were not even human beings. We all felt pretty sad."

"I will never make girls feel sad. We were talking about Italian jewelry," said Xiaomin.

"I'm sure Mr. Shi is going to buy excellent jewelry for you." Linda picked up the tray, saying, "He's a successful businessman. A couple of jewels don't cost him much. He owns a big house in Hongqiao. Am I right? I've got to go. Let's take these devils."

Xiaomin laughed so much that she bent down on the counter.

"What did the other girl say?" asked Mr. Shi.

"She was singing," said Xiaomin.

At lunchtime the hospital's dining hall was full of

people in white gowns.

Xiaomin and An'an were standing in line. Both of them had a happy smile. Somebody said to Xiaomin, "Now, your partner has come back."

"Don't use that word. We're not homosexual partners," An'an said while waving to the nurse.

An'an took out something from her breast pocket. She said to Xiaomin smilingly, "Do you know what I found at home?"

Xiaomin flashed her bright eyes at her, saying, "What?"

"Did you lose something? Why are you so frightened?"

Xiaomin noticed An'an was staring at her.

All of a sudden, An'an cracked a smile and said, "I'm teasing you. Why are you so timid?" She opened her hand and Xiaomin's butterfly-shaped ring was lying on her palm. "I found it in our bathroom."

Xiaomin pinched An'an's arm and said through clenched teeth, "It was rough of you to frighten me like that. I was tired out when I helped decorate your damned home. While you were out there making meaningful contributions, I was helping you by buying curtains. I was afraid that the curtain might be too small, so I had to soak it in your bathtub. The curtain almost broke up my ring. The thick curtain is good for blocking sunlight. When it is drawn during the day, your room will be as dark as at night. But the wet curtain was so heavy. What's more, I helped hang your picture frame. Alas, you even blamed me for that." With these words she took over her ring and put it on her middle finger. She spread her hand, saying, "Pay me the service charge."

An'an reached out her hand and said with a smile, "I know you've done me a big favor." She spread her palm to reveal a snake-shaped silver ankle chain, saying, "Here you are. It matches your beautiful foot."

"Did you buy it?" Xiaomin bent her head and took the soft, brilliant ankle chain from An'an's hand. She raised it closer and had a good look at it.

"Do you think I stole it?" said An'an.

"It was stupid of you to buy such an expensive thing." Xiaomin gave An'an a shove.

An'an dodged nimbly and protected the soup she had just bought. Xiaomin put the ankle chain in her breast pocket. After she bought her lunch, they took their food and sat down at a sunny table near the window.

An'an said, "Can you guess why I bought a present like that for you? It's because of the curtain. When I approached the front door of my house, I caught sight of the bright colored curtain drying on the balcony. You're worthy of the name 'best friend' because the curtain you chose was exactly what I liked. When I was working in the countryside, I was worried that Little Chen might choose the wrong color. Now, its silvery color perfectly matches the pink wall. I was also worried that Little Chen might forget to immerse the cloth and end up with a curtain which was too small. As soon as I saw the cloth hanging out on the balcony, I felt greatly relieved. I knew very well Little Chen was not capable of that. It must have been your outstanding work. The minute I put down my baggage, I went to buy this present for you."

An'an bent down and patted Xiaomin on the side, saying, "The ankle chain will set off your slender long legs very well. When you sit cross-legged at the bar, people can see it. The Taiwanese bumpkin will be bewitched by you."

Xiaomin bent her head to eat the soup. All of a sudden, she was choked by the soup and started coughing. She coughed so much that she blushed deeply.

An'an stopped eating and cast a glance at her, saying, "Why are you in a hurry? Nobody will take the food from you."

Xiaomin had a coughing fit and felt like vomiting. Tears blurred her eyes. She looked at An'an sitting in the sunlight. An'an was staring at her with an innocent look. An'an had a deeply contoured face typical of a southern girl. The sunshine used to produce many shadows on it. However, right there and then, An'an's face looked bright and beautiful. Xiaomin finally stopped coughing and said, "Your words are too fulsome. People who have overheard your remark will suspect that we are lovers."

5

The days were dragging on as if nothing unusual had happened. Xiaomin gradually lost her sense of guilt.

Xiaomin no longer felt embarrassed when she and An'an were in each other's company. In her mind, she let bygones be bygones. If An'an had learned about the fact, she would have become needlessly upset. As a matter of fact, this well-kept secret would not do An'an any harm. Thus, Xiaomin found a convenient excuse to appease her conscience. Xiaomin put her heart at rest when she and An'an got along as well as usual. Finally, she did wear the snake-shaped ankle chain when she went to the bar. Some people said it looked seductively beautiful. Sometimes Xiaomin and An'an went home together after they got off work.

It seemed as if the days were going on by blotting out people's memory of many past events. Nevertheless, one morning marked a turning point. Early one morning Xiaomin received an internal call from An'an. She asked her to go to her ward area and she had something urgent to tell her.

An'an showed Xiaomin to the nurses' dressing room. The room was hung with a variety of beautiful clothes. There was a bunk bed used by the nurses on night duty to get some sleep. They sat down on the lower berth.

Xiaomin said, "What's so urgent?"

"There's something wrong with Little Chen." Xiaomin's spirits sank when she heard An'an's abrupt remark. She was at a loss for words and focused her eyes on An'an. An'an raised her fair-complexioned face and stared at her, saying, "I'm sure he had an affair when I was away."

"How do you know?"

"My instinct tells me. The night when I came back from the countryside, I found he had changed. He used to make sweet talk with me after we made love. Now he is very practical. He used to say we were the best, most loving couple on earth. He looked like a landlord who was inspecting the grain in his field. But recently, at night, he said I had acted like a log and I was lacking in emotional appeal. Later, I noticed movement on his side of the bed when I woke up at midnight. As we share the same mattress, his stirring disturbed me. To my surprise, he was masturbating. I had never seen him masturbate before. I'm certain there is something wrong with him."

"I don't think so," Xiaomin begged to differ. When she listened to An'an, she recalled her lovemaking with Little Chen. It brought some comfort to her. With the gradual rising of a warm feeling, she even felt secretly delighted.

"Do you know what Little Chen was doing while I was away?"

"How could I know?" Xiaomin was so shocked that her warm feeling disappeared completely. She was annoyed with herself for being jealous of her best friend at such a moment.

"There must be a slut who got involved."

Xiaomin noticed An'an's determination to unearth the suspected woman. For the first time Xiaomin observed that when the usually amiable An'an pulled a long face, her curved eyes became two big black holes which exuded a quiet cold. Xiaomin had never seen An'an behave so oddly. Xiaomin became terribly upset and restless. But she soon gave An'an a push and forced her to lie down on the quilt. She said, "Don't put on a frosty look like that. How come you're so unreasonably suspicious?"

"How do you know I'm unreasonably suspicious? That's a woman's intuition."

Xiaomin said, "You can't suspect him without

any proof. Perhaps ... yes, I recall one thing. When we went to shop for the curtain, I saw a porn videotape in his briefcase. He said he had to watch this kind of stuff while you were not at home."

"Really?"

"That's true. Why should I stand by your husband's side? Nowadays, most men are womanizers. If a man doesn't have this kind of experience, he will be looked down upon. If a woman is not good at making love, she will not be able to keep her husband's affection. Do you still think we live in the old days when men liked women who knew very little about love-making? Times have changed."

"Really?" An'an cast a glance at Xiaomin. "Where are we going to learn those obscene skills?"

"Obscene skills? That's a woman's sexual appeal. Haven't you read this kind of discussion column in the magazines? The host of the midnight program of the radio station also talked about this subject. He sounded like a pimp."

Then they chatted about the magazines they had read and the radio programs they had listened to. They finally concluded that since they were brought up to be pure and abstinent, they had now fallen behind the times and become ignorant women in the present age.

In the old days a woman was required to be ferocious enough to tame her husband. Nowadays, women were required to have sex appeal to capture men. Now women were aiming to become flowers instead of fighters. Today's mature women were brought up in an atmosphere where desire was suppressed. They had no idea how to display their sexual appeal. That's why women's magazines devoted so much space to the discussion of this subject.

Xiaomin said that the most appealing women were the bar girls who could earn a lot of money by simply smiling and chatting. "Whores attract men with their bodies, but the bar girls don't sell their bodies. Of course, their dressing is sometimes frightening. In my mind, a woman should attach importance to her dressing."

"As the times have changed, women should please men first before they can ride roughshod over them," Xiaomin concluded.

"I've misjudged Little Chen. He appears honest,

but actually he is full of craft and guile." An'an half believed what she had said. "He must have a taste for some more appealing women. Otherwise he would not complain that I was lacking in emotional appeal."

"He may have gained some experience by watching the porn videotape."

"If he's not satisfied, neither am I. I don't mind a divorce. He can choose any woman he likes. If he catches a venereal disease, he can go and see one of those experienced military doctors recommended on the advertisements pasted on street poles. I can find my Mr. Right. I'll go with you and work as a barmaid."

Xiaomin patted An'an gently on the shoulder, saying, "Don't be crazy. It's difficult for girls of our age to find an ideal man. Fine men are in great demand. There won't be any left for us. If it had been easy to choose a prospective partner, I would not have gone to that kind of place every day."

"That's true. Even you can't find an ideal one, to say nothing of me." An'an nodded her head.

"I will never beg him to stop it," said An'an. "Maybe you can go and talk with him."

Xiaomin said, "How did you come up with such

an absurd idea? How can I talk with him about your private matter?"

Xiaomin stared at An'an, saying, "I didn't ask you to plead with him for mercy. Do you think I'm so stupid? We'll see to it that he will come and beg you. Your Little Chen is a mature man. What he demands is a sexy woman instead of a virgin. If you give full play to your sexual appeal, those young girls will be no match for you."

An'an gave a snigger and said, "It seems to me you're an expert in this respect. How many boyfriends have you got?"

"Are you out of your mind? I'm giving you some good advice." When she saw An'an crack a smile, Xiaomin felt relieved and became herself again. "Look at your hairstyle," she said while pulling An'an's bang. "You look like an innocent little girl. Your hairstyle is out of style." She pulled open An'an's collar and looked downward. An'an yelled and covered up her blouse. Xiaomin said, "You should change your underwear, too. All sorts of underwear are on display in the shops. Why don't you go and buy some?" Xiaomin said with a grin, "After you change yourself, Little Chen will come and plead with you for mercy. Then you should order him to kneel down and kowtow to you. It's a piece of cake to deal with men."

An'an suddenly pulled open Xiaomin's collar and saw a black laced bra closely fitting her body. Xiaomin uttered a sound of surprise and covered up her blouse immediately, saying, "How shameless you are!"

"Let's copy your model," An'an said with a smile.

They acted swiftly and resolutely. An'an and Xiaomin changed their shift with other nurses and got two hours off. They went to the Huating Isetan Department Store. There were no other customers in the underwear department on the second floor. With the soft background music coming from the overhead hi-fi system, they walked past a big pottery pot of brilliant and colorful flowers and came to the bra section. The black bra displayed on the dummy looked exactly the same as Xiaomin's.

"This type is fashionable," Xiaomin said while looking at it.

"There are so many foreign shops in Shanghai that I can't visit them all. But in this shop I don't see many customers."

"They sell expensive goods here. I like it for this reason. We don't need to squeeze through the crowd," said Xiaomin.

"You really know your stuff."

"Yes, I do like this shop. When I go shopping here, I feel like I live a decent life. I bought your curtain here. There's a café on the top floor where shoppers can take a break. There's an exotic atmosphere in the café. You'll feel like you are sitting in any high-class overseas café like the ones in foreign magazines," said Xiaomin.

An'an settled on a flesh-colored nightgown with a fine lace ornament on its front. She pointed it out to Xiaomin and the salesgirl brought them one immediately. They went to the fitting room. An'an unfolded the nightgown in front of her to see whether it fitted her body. Leaning against the door, Xiaomin said in a casual manner, "Don't act like an innocent girl, your idea requires change and effort."

With these words Xiaomin passed the black nightgown in her hand to An'an, saying, "I think this one is better. You see its lace trimmings are transparent."

An'an unfolded the black one in front of her. When she looked at herself in the mirror, she was pale with fright. She put it down, saying, "I'll look like a slut wearing this nightgown."

"You'll look sexy!" shouted Xiaomin. "An'an, don't forget your reason for shopping. You should keep in mind what your Little Chen likes, and what will make his heart throb. The nightgown isn't for your sake, but for his sake. Do you understand?"

"Do you know what color a bad man likes most?" An'an asked while glancing at Xiaomin in the mirror.

"Black," said Xiaomin while looking at An'an in the mirror. "I learned from the statistics I read in a book that many men have sexual urges when they see women in black underwear." Xiaomin imitated a man's sexual urge. An'an could not help laughing. She said, "Damn it, Little Chen is going to like this."

An'an spread out the black nightgown again in front of her. She looked at herself in the mirror and said in a hesitant tone, "OK, I'll take it."

After shopping, Xiaomin and An'an went to Xiaomin's room. Because of its convenience for going to work at night, Xiaomin rented a small room between two flights of stairs in a typical *shikumen* house. The girls came in from the back door and passed through a public kitchen. The layers of grey yellowish soot piled up on the wall looked like stalactite. They groped their way along the dark hallway and came to the stairs. When they climbed up the age-old wood stairs, a loud creak followed them all the way up. When she came back home at midnight, Xiaomin always climbed the stairs close to the handrail and avoided stepping on the middle part of the worn staircase.

In the afternoon sunlight a cloud of dust could be seen flying over the ancient stairs. The old-fashioned grandfather clock was striking the hour upstairs. Hearing the chiming of the clock, both of them looked upward.

An old woman appeared at the top of the staircase. Her tiny pale face looked like an aged basket hanging above the stairs. She was so old that her eyelids and nose were drooping like cotton. However feeble, the old woman was still on full alert.

As soon as the she caught sight of them, Xiaomin and An'an greeted her in unison, "Granny Wang!"

The old woman felt relieved and said, "Is it time for you to get off work? The sun is still high in the sky."

An'an said, "We have the day off today."

"An'an, I know you went to the countryside to provide emergency medical aid. Xiaomin came back very late those days. When she went to the night school, no matter how late she came back, I could hear her steps. She was very busy decorating your house, I could hardly hear her steps at night. You're best friends, and since Xiaomin is my tenant and lives alone here, I have to show concern for her safety. Nowadays there are more and more wicked men."

"Since An'an is back home, I won't take charge of anymore decorating." Xiaomin said while flashing a glance at An'an. An'an was focusing her eyes on her in the dark.

Xiaomin pretended to pay no attention to the old woman's remarks. She shrugged her shoulders and fumbled in her purse for the keys. She opened the door hurriedly and pulled An'an inside. To her surprise, the old woman followed them closely. She said, "Xiaomin, you came back very late last night. Your grandma came to visit you and waited for a long time in my room. Your grandma looked very young. If she had not told me, I would have thought it was your mom who came to see you from Qingpu."

Xiaomin cast a stare at the old woman and kept silent.

"Your grandma asked me why you went to night school every day and why you did not come back home even at 10 o'clock. I told her you would not come back until midnight. In the old days, a dancing-girl lived in our lane. She came back at midnight every day and all the neighbors could hear the heavy footsteps of her leather-soled shoes."

Xiaomin stared at the old woman with a forced smile, but with a fierce look.

The old woman changed the topic of her conversation, "As we're in new times now, young girls come back late because they attend the night school. Things are different now."

Xiaomin turned about, pulled An'an into her room and closed the door. She said to An'an, "As the old woman stays at home alone all day long, she becomes unbearably talkative whenever she meets somebody."

The window of Xiaomin's room was wide open.

The mattress was covered with a neat quilt and a white embroidered bed cover. Even the area rug was placed in neat order. All her clothes were hung on a long stainless steel rod like those used by many garment shops and they were shielded by a big piece of white cloth.

Xiaomin did not have a trunk or a wardrobe. She hung all her clothes for various seasons on the clothing rod. When An'an asked her why she did not buy a wardrobe, she said she was awaiting her future husband to buy a mahogany one.

Every time An'an paid Xiaomin a visit, she would feel as if Xiaomin was ready to move house. Every time she came back home from her visit to Xiaomin, An'an ended up with a better opinion of her own home. As a result, An'an often tried to persuade Xiaomin to marry a "just about right" man instead of wasting her youth waiting for Mr. Right. But this time she was here to resolve her own family crisis.

Xiaomin took off her high-heeled shoes on the rug. She lifted her foot and massaged her toes.

"Did you really do a painstaking job?" asked An'an.

"What?"

"For decorating my new house. But I don't see why you needed to spend the whole night purchasing a curtain."

"Of course I didn't. My neighbors don't know I work at the bar. When the old woman asked me why I came back so late, I had to provide a convenient excuse." Xiaomin bent down to massage her toes attentively.

An'an cracked a smile, saying, "Unfortunately, you are paying rent only to get yourself another Grandma."

Xiaomin said, "I can assure you that I'll buy a big house some day and I won't let anybody poke their nose into my business anymore."

An'an said, "I'm afraid only your Taiwanese friend can help you. I read in the newspaper that most Taiwanese businessmen working in the mainland have wives in Taiwan and are anxious to find a concubine here. You have to be careful not to become just an accessory for them."

"Do you think I'm so stupid?" Xiaomin bent down to put her shoes aside. "Anyway, mind your own business. Take out your new clothes."

An'an took out her new underwear from the bag. She unfolded the nightgown in front of her and looked at herself in the mirror. She said, "Tonight when I walk into the room after I take a bath, he will be frightened out of his wits at seeing me wearing such a nightgown." "That's exactly what he deserves. Only then will he discover your glamour and charm." With these words, Xiaomin lay down on the bed and rested her chin on her chest, saying, "Let's have a rehearsal. I can see whether you are going to produce a really dramatic effect. You know I have a keen eye for this. Now I'll play the role of your Little Chen." The minute she uttered these remarks, she got up, drew the curtain and turned on the bedside lamp. "Look, a soft light like this will do. Do remember to turn on the bedside lamp beside your big bed. Its pinkish light will suit the occasion. The bright light will eliminate a certain mystery."

An'an hid herself behind Xiaomin's clothing rod. She poked her smiling face while changing her clothes. She said, "You picked up bad habits by working at the bar. You see what dirty tricks you've learned."

"That means I know the ways of the world."

Xiaomin lay down again and assumed her previous position.

Clad in her black nightgown, An'an stepped from behind the clothing rod. She looked at her own legs and touched her own body, saying, "Oh my! My bottom is exposed."

"Good! You're his wife. You have nothing to fear from him," said Xiaomin. "Please relax. Why do you have to behave weirdly? Don't shrug your shoulders."

"That strap is falling off." An'an was clutching the two thin straps on her shoulders.

"Just let it fall. Didn't you see the foreign girl on the advertisement? It's fashionable to let one strap fall. Let go of it. Walk up here the way you did at home." Xiaomin waved at her. "Little Chen was watching you while lying on the big bed. He's always waiting for you to get into bed."

An'an let her strap go. She stepped sideways and the strap slipped off her shoulder. She ignored it after a brief hesitation and moved another step in this way.

Xiaomin exploded with laughter, saying, "You're acting like a crab who always moves sideways."

An'an was bent over with helpless laughter, saying, "That's your fault. I was so nervous that I didn't know how to walk normally."

"Do it again, do it again!" Xiaomin urged.

An'an straightened up and looked at Xiaomin. Xiaomin rested her chin on her chest and fixed her smiling eyes on An'an. Her lower lip was slightly protruding.

An idea flashed across An'an's mind and she shouted by pointing at Xiaomin, "Little Chen often lies on the bed exactly like that. Your posture looks exactly like his."

After An'an left for home, Xiaomin planned to take a rest before she went to the bar. She lay sprawled across the bed. When she opened her legs, she thought of Little Chen. She had a sense that those days were gone forever. Xiaomin turned over in bed and began to think of her bar, Mr. Shi and his cousin. She was pondering over the possible link between them and her future.

She was not as fragile as she looked. When one illusion of hers was shattered, she would straighten herself out and set a new goal so as to get her strengths back into full play. But, she never poured out her heart to others.

While lying on the bed, she detected the smell of braised pork seasoned with soy sauce drifting up from the old woman's kitchen. She recalled the days spent at Grandma's. Grandma often cooked this kind of pork for Grandpa because he was a real meat addict. Xiaomin saw in her mind's eye a big bowl of steaming braised pork on an old round mahogany table, Grandma's table, sofa, and standing lamp behind the sofa, and the yellowish light emitted from the gauze lampshade, all of which was typical of a well-off family then.

Xiaomin's parents got acquainted with each other when they left their native city and settled in the countryside. They sent their baby girl Xiaomin to Grandma's home in Shanghai for fear that their daughter might fall into the bad habits of the country folk. So Xiaomin was brought up by her Grandma. After working hard for a dozen years, her parents finally managed to move from An'hui Province back to Qingpu—one of the ten suburban counties of Shanghai. Of course, their future was very bleak.

Every time Xiaomin met them, a line of poetry would spring to her mind, i.e., "ten thousand saplings shoot up beyond the withered tree." Her mother spent her youth in the countryside and now looked even older than Grandma.

Xiaomin always felt that really she belonged to Grandma's home. She was reluctant to admit that she disliked her own mother. She only paid occasional visits to her parents in Qingpu. Whenever she saw her mother, she would be shocked to see that no trace of Grandma's graceful bearing could be found in her mother, who seemed to be a stranger to her and Grandma. She moved out of Grandma's home on the pretext that she had to study English at night and prepare for overseas nurse training. Her mother was so block-headed that she never suspected her motives. Grandma however made a routine check on her every other day. Xiaomin was aware that Grandma was afraid she might cohabit with some boy. If Xiaomin wasted the prime of her youth, it would be difficult for her to marry an ideal man.

Xiaomin jumped up from the bed and went to Grandma's home.

Grandma was sorting out mung beans in front of the window. She looked at Xiaomin and said, "You're giving off a coquettish scent like a dancing-girl. Where on earth do you moonlight? I wonder whether you're really too fully occupied to come back home." Xiaomin took out a can of crackers. She sat down on the sofa and started eating them slowly, deliberately. She gave Grandma a cold stare and said, "What's wrong with being a dancing-girl? Those girls are rich now. They're making a fortune by relying on their own efforts. They don't need to dream of marrying a rich man like me."

From what she had heard, Grandma seemed convinced that Xiaomin was doing nothing wrong. She bent her head and continued to sort out mung beans. She said, "Nowadays, girls use such vulgar language."

"You're right. Nowadays, nothing is really good. That's why we need to reinvigorate Shanghai."

Xiaomin reached into the can and searched for something, saying, "Last time I told you to buy Sullivan crackers. How do they taste?"

"Awful. They don't taste as good as before, but

they have the audacity to use the Sullivan brand."
Grandma shook her head, saying, "Nowadays, people
are low and shameless."

"Right now, everything popular in your times
becomes fashionable again. The out-turned hairstyle
you used to wear is the most fashionable for young
girls. It seems that they follow your classic example in
everything they do now."

"In my time that was the hairstyle for married
women. It's silly for young girls to imitate that style.
Even if people want to imitate our classic styles, it
will be neither fish nor fowl. In my time Shanghai
was the oriental Paris. What are you now? You're like
nude people wearing a tie." Grandma could not help
laughing herself.

Xiaomin hated Grandma most for uttering
such remarks. She felt downcast. It reminded her of
being overtaken by other runners in the long-distance
races when she was a student. She would lag behind
so far that she could never catch up with them. Even
if she and other runners were running on the same
racetrack, they were worlds apart in ability. She bent
her head and concentrated her attention on eating

crackers. "Why don't you go to work?" said Grandma.

"I'm not interested. Every time I see the ward, I will feel terribly upset. The patients are dirty, ugly, disgusting and impoverished. Nowadays, patients are really low and shameless. There's no comparison between them and Grandpa," said Xiaomin.

"Even though you're not assigned to work in the ward area for foreign patients, you don't need to hate the hospital like this. Nursing is your career and you should respect your job. It's not good for a woman to be full of hatred. If she has a deep hatred, her face will darken." Grandma cast a stare at Xiaomin.

Xiaomin was scared and straightened up. She said with irritation, "Grandma, please don't frighten me with these words. As the hospital has been allotted quotas for sending nurses abroad, I have to study English at a night school in order to pass the English test. I'm making every effort to shape my future." Xiaomin cast a stare at Grandma and said, "I'm not as lucky as somebody who can find a good husband by giving him injections. As I have no rich husband to support me, I have to endure years of suffering."

Grandma was amused by her complaint. She

pointed at Xiaomin, saying, "Your impetuous manner will frighten away any promise of a good husband."

Xiaomin said, "Grandma, can we swap roles? I wish I were old enough to ignore the whole damned issue of marriage."

Right there and then she saw Grandma's face light up with satisfaction. Grandma's clean face glowed like a piece of pure jade because she sensed she was gaining the upper hand. Xiaomin could not reconcile herself to the pride people of Grandma's generation felt. They bragged about the days they had spent in the past in the presence of Xiaomin's generation who had a sincere desire to learn from them, follow their example and almost reproduce their life. They teased young girls like Xiaomin as if they were tantalizing pet cats and puppies with a colored ball. When they became eager to get it, the old ladies would remind them that it was beyond their reach.

Xiaomin said immediately, "I refuse to resign myself to fate. I want to find a richer husband than Grandpa. I want to have an authentic American as my husband and he will buy me a big house furnished with everything American. I don't want to worship a lamp all my life. I don't like to live with second-hand furniture."

When a smile froze on Grandma's face, Xiaomin burst into laughter. She jumped up from the sofa and smoothed out her clothes. She said, "I've got to go. There will be classes tonight."

6

The next day Xiaomin received an internal call from An'an the minute she arrived at the office. An'an said, "I'm on my way to the operating room. It's a minor operation for appendectomy." An'an said hurriedly, "You know what?"

"What?" asked Xiaomin.

"Last night that unpredictable lamp did not work even if Little Chen tried his best to turn it on. This morning he crawled under the bed and found the lamp was disconnected with the mains when he pushed the suitcase in. How unlucky I was!"

"How did Little Chen react?"

"He didn't see me in my nightgown. When he

noticed it by fumbling about in the bed, he said, did you receive a bonus and buy masses of lace to sleep in? He also said that my lacy nightgown felt like fish scales. He was out of his mind and said it's a reward for my efforts for going to work in the disaster area." An'an could not help laughing herself. She continued, "Do you think he is out of his mind?"

"Did he say that you looked sexy?" asked Xiaomin.

"Not a single comment, because the lamp did not work." All of a sudden, An'an gave a brief reply to somebody else. She said to Xiaomin over the phone again, "I'm going to the operating room. We'll have lunch together."

When they ate their lunch, Xiaomin and An'an sat at the same table as before. An'an waved her soup spoon in front of her face, saying, "The lamp wasn't working so we couldn't see each other."

Xiaomin said, "You were really unlucky."

"After Little Chen made the comment, I touched my nightgown and it did feel like fish scales."

"Do remember to check the lamp before you go to bed tonight. Anyway, now that he has associated it with fish scales, I don't think it will work anymore," said Xiaomin.

"The real reason why he behaved like that is there is no more chemistry between us. If he had met a new girl, or if he had met you, he would have been panting for breath."

"Are you crazy? You're making fun of me. If I were some other girl, I would probably slap you!" Xiaomin said agitatedly.

However, An'an did not mind. Shining through the window, the sun cast shadows of motley shapes on An'an's face. You could catch a trace of a worried smile on her face. She had a blank expression as if she had been let down. Xiaomin thought, a woman who enjoys her home life will certainly take a matter to heart if her husband betrays her. Nowadays people lack that kind of security.

However, she saw in her mind's eye that Little Chen took their brief love affair seriously. She had encountered many men at the bar who had women other than their spouse and who took no heed of faithfulness. Xiaomin did not expect that any man would act against the principle that "things change with the passage of time." Little Chen still harbored lovesick feelings toward her at the expense of his own family life. How could the relationship between Little Chen and her ever work out well? These days a single slip could cause a lifetime of sorrow. She had no intention of bringing that kind of grief to Little Chen, his family and An'an. What's more, it wouldn't do her any good either.

Xiaomin decided she would rather give herself a good beating for acting so foolishly and gain nothing at the expense of her best friendship. She made up her mind to help An'an.

An'an spoke her thoughts aloud, "Last night I thought that he had had an affair. And that since he has another woman, he doesn't care about me. And I found he deliberately compared my nightgown to fish scales. He knew that I had changed into the nightgown and he uttered a remark like that to hurt me on purpose. If there weren't an attractive woman on his mind, he would not have turned me down like this because he's a man who never tired of lovemaking. There must be another woman between us."

"I'm shocked by your frightening talk." Xiaomin

bent her head and focused her attention on separating fish flesh from fish bones with her tongue. Then she opened her mouth and took out the fish bones.

"I'm sure he doesn't have a woman with him every day."

"How do you know?" An'an fixed her eyes on her.

Xiaomin was dumbfounded. She was aware she had made a slip of the tongue. But how could she tell the truth? It would have helped if he had more than one woman. She blamed Little Chen for being too conventional.

She knew An'an was waiting for her answer. But she was at a loss for words. She feigned having fish bones in the mouth and put her fingers into her mouth.

A moment later she said, "Your Little Chen is always cautious. It can't be easy for him now that he's been promoted. How can he have an affair? What's more, he is not rich. Nowadays, having an affair costs a lot of money. You hold the purse strings at home. Since he has only a little pocket money, no woman would court a man without taking material gains into consideration."

An'an remained silent while staring at Xiaomin.

Xiaomin said, "Let's not make things complicated. Even if he has another woman, if I were you, I would try my best to win him over. If you like, you can dump him in future. But you will lose face if you are outsmarted by another woman and fail to win back the affection of your own husband."

"It's better to have a divorce. Once we go to court, the policemen will locate her, whoever she is, by any means. Let them get married. I don't think it will be a glorious page in their history," said An'an.

"Are you out of your mind? Why should you hand your own husband over to another woman?" Xiaomin was resolutely opposed to the idea. She fastened her eyes on An'an and then said, "It's strange that you talked about a divorce. Do you really want a divorce?"

Tears welled up in An'an's eyes. She looked at Xiaomin and said with a sense of grievance, "Fancy a confidante like you not knowing my real feelings!"

Xiaomin was frightened by An'an's tears. She looked around and, fortunately, nobody was paying any attention to them. She took out the sterilized gauze from her breast pocket and handed it over to An'an. She said, "I made a slip of the tongue. That's my fault. Your expression is so frightening that other people may think there's something wrong with us."

An'an said in a fit of pique, "My husband wants to dump me. I tried my best to ingratiate myself with him, but he remains indifferent. Something must have gone wrong. When he woke up this morning, he lay on the bed the way you did last time and glared at me. Do you know what he said to me? He said my nightgown felt like the scales of a snakehead fish. You can guess that I lost my self-respect completely."

"What's the use of crying?" said Xiaomin.

"What can I do if I don't cry?" An'an covered her eyes and let out a bitter sob.

They hurried over their lunch and came to a secluded corner of the hospital's garden. They sat down and started to discuss how to deal with an unfaithful man.

According to Xiaomin, "The traditional way of crying, making a scene and threatening to commit suicide wouldn't work anymore. The more terrible the scene you make, the more you will give him a handle against you. A woman in modern times should learn how to steal a man's heart and make him hang on her every word. In a magazine survey I read they asked what kind of woman was the most charming, most men answered that men should be tough while women should be gentle. A gentle woman should be obedient and tactful. A woman should show due respect to her husband's dignity in public while keeping him under her control in private."

An'an said, "Then what about the liberation of women?"

Xiaomin waved to An'an, saying, "Times have changed. Do you think it's still a sin for a man to lead a dissipated life? Nowadays, if a man concludes that you're not what he wants in a woman, you'll be hopeless. Even those white-collar office ladies with a large income have their lips brightly rouged, to say nothing of us poor nurses."

Finally, An'an said through clenched teeth, "I don't think I'm incapable of acting as a gentle woman. I'm not ugly at all."

Xiaomin said, "That's true. To be frank, I think

it will be beneath your dignity to try every means to ingratiate yourself with Little Chen."

They decided to try again.

When they parted, Xiaomin gave An'an another piece of advice, "When you go back home, do remember to bring a bottle of wine with you. Wine is a good sex appetizer."

In the dead of night Xiaomin came back home from the bar. She used facial tissue to wipe off her eye-liner in the lamplight. After cleaning her face, she showed no signs of tiredness. Instead, she looked young and delighted.

Light music was coming from the portable recorder on the table.

She looked at herself carefully in the mirror. She took out a long and thin red box from her purse. She opened it and pulled out a necklace inlaid with artificial diamonds—a gift from Mr. Shi. Mr. Shi paid a family visit to Taiwan and brought his cousin to Shanghai. His tall and thin cousin looked like a gentleman and spoke Taiwanese Chinese. He reminded Xiaomin of a character in Chiung Yao's novels. She learned from Mr. Shi that his cousin earned more money than he. As the cousin had divorced recently and was anxious to leave the land of sorrow, he planned to open a factory in Shanghai.

Xiaomin noticed he was drinking wine in sips. He was a quiet man with cleanly polished nails. Shanghai people speak Mandarin with a local accent. Their exaggerated pronunciation gives a vulgar impression. Northerners speak Mandarin in such a domineering tone that they sound like bandits. Neither was to her liking, but Xiaomin was fascinated by his strange and familiar Taiwanese Chinese. However, he did not talk much with her and was very polite. After he saw Mr. Shi gave her a necklace as a gift, he gave her 50 US dollars as a tip when he left the bar.

As the bar was filled with customers, Xiaomin did not have time to think much about it.

She put the necklace in front of her chest. It was sparkling like real diamonds. She unhooked it and put it on. The necklace was a bit too long so that she pulled down her collar to reveal the pendant. She examined herself carefully in the mirror and found the girl with a necklace on was different from her usual self. She raised her chin slightly.

Something was not right.

It was the close-fitting blouse. It did not match the classic necklace.

Xiaomin stood up and searched through the clothes hanging on the rod. Finally, she selected a red blouse and replaced the black one she was wearing.

She heard a strange sound. She paused and listened attentively.

It was so quiet as if the whole building was asleep. The rumbling of the big trucks could be heard from the distant street.

She heard somebody tapping at the door with nails.

Xiaomin jumped up and slipped on her blouse before she opened the door.

It was none other than Little Chen, who stepped sideways through the door breathy with alcohol.

"Why are you here?" Xiaomin buttoned up hurriedly. But at heart she was not ashamed of being scantily clad, because they had slept together.

"I miss you." Little Chen stepped forward as if he was going to embrace Xiaomin. Xiaomin moved backward and pointed to the chair at the table, saying,

"Go and sit there."

Little Chen went over and sat down, saying, "I've waited at the gate of your house for the whole night. I miss you very much." With these words Little Chen held up something in his hand. With the aid of the lamplight, Xiaomin saw in his hand a wrapped rose, a red rose encircled by a small bunch of white baby's breath.

"Didn't we have an agreement to avoid behaving like high school students?" said Xiaomin.

"Yes. But I had never expected that I was not capable of real intimacy with An'an after she came back. Whenever I touch her, I think of you. I want you. I don't know how she came up with the idea, but she bought the same black nightgown as yours. I could only bear her by pretending to sleep with you. But she did not give off the nice smell of the bar as you did. I'm immensely fond of that smell."

"How could you behave like that?" Xiaomin was exasperated. "Do you forget completely how assiduously you were courting An'an?"

"To tell you the truth. I was clear about what had happened. It seemed as if I was courting her.

But in fact I fell into a trap she had laid. She was so thoughtful that she acted like a log in bed. She's craftier than before and even feigns orgasms. I can see through her deceptions. She is no match for you. I've experienced so much that I won't buy into her tricks. Every night she has lust in her eyes when she looks at me. Her look is really frightening."

"What excuse did you make up for leaving An'an?"

"I told her that I had to go to the office to wait for a fax, a fax sent from America."

"I can no longer have an affair with you," Xiaomin said while pulling a long face.

"Simply because you're best friends?" Little Chen pulled a long face, too. Xiaomin noticed his cheekbones had become higher and he looked undernourished. He was so poor and so shameless. Xiaomin regretted having had an affair with him.

"One has to act according to one's conscience. I hate to see your family broken up."

"It's not you who came to grab me. It's I who want you."

"I don't want you."

"How come you have such a short memory?"

"I have to live a decent life. If we maintain a close liaison, it'll be impossible for me to live a decent life. I don't want to make that kind of sacrifice," said Xiaomin.

In the lamplight Little Chen fixed his eyes on Xiaomin, saying, "Nowadays, it's common to have an affair. How can a bit of gossip prevent a barmaid from living a decent life? Perhaps, in the very beginning you decided to play fast and loose with my affections. I was under the false impression that you were in love with me."

"I really can't do that." Xiaomin said in a mild tone. "OK, I won't talk about a decent life. Just compare An'an with me. She is prettier than I. Almost every year a couple of interns take a fancy to her. Is it news to you? As for me, I've worked at the bar for a long time and I'm not the type who will pledge enduring affection. If you marry me, I will probably make you a cuckold. It will be no fun and end in tears."

Xiaomin spoke eloquently engaging morality, appearance and temperament to try to persuade Little Chen to give up the idea. In the end Little Chen put the withering rose on the table and said before leaving, "I hope you'll ponder carefully. I've fallen in love with you. If you don't want to get married, we can be secret lovers. But you're not supposed to dump me."

Xiaomin understood she was in trouble. An'an was determined to hunt the mysterious foxy woman, while Little Chen was willing to wait until midnight to present her with a rose. An'an was talking about getting a divorce and he had no desire to touch his wife. None of this could be beneficial to her.

Right there and then Xiaomin felt she would never marry Little Chen. Nor would she waste a single day of her youth for his sake. How could she know that Little Chen was so narrow-minded and prone to overestimating his own abilities?

7

Xiaomin and An'an walked slowly on the street while licking ice cream. Like all the other Shanghai women, they ate their ice cream quickly and steadily with small bites. They used the torn-off wrapper to cover the ice cream carefully. As a result, no melted ice cream dropped down and the rouge on their lips remained intact.

Xiaomin said, "Next time we'll enjoy the American ice cream sold on Nanjing Road. It tastes better than our home-made ice cream. What's more, it's not sticky."

An'an uttered a sound of agreement.

An'an was wearing a clinging gown-shaped dress. Her new hairstyle was distinguished by the protruding moussed fringe. She was walking gingerly by Xiaomin's side. She was smiling while stealing glances at the passers-by. Her manner, both timid and formal, reflected her uncertainty about her attire. She did not feel comfortable and was afraid people would find out. That's why she was walking in an awkward manner. She looked as if she were a girl born in a small town who came to visit Shanghai for the first time.

She swallowed the ice cream. She pouted her lips and showed the bright red lipstick to Xiaomin, saying, "I've never used this kind of color. I don't like it because your lips look so red—as if you had just eaten a dead baby."

Xiaomin comforted her by saying, "The bar girls all look like this. Since Little Chen blamed you for acting like a log, you just go and show him what evil tricks you can play. As long as you sit in the corner of the bar for the whole night, your hair will be filled with the smell of the bar. That's the place he dare not step in. Though he's a civil servant full of craft and guile, he dare not visit a place like that. But he's the type of person who has an insatiable curiosity." She cast a glance at An'an. An'an was so excited that her big eyes were shining in the yellowish light of the street lamps. She had a very vivid expression on her face. Xiaomin nudged her playfully, saying, "You look much prettier than the bar girls. Your coyness may attract a big businessman because the bar girls are too thick-skinned and shameless."

"I wonder why you seem to know so well what goes on in Little Chen's mind. How do you know Little Chen likes the smell of your bar?"

"I don't mean the smell of our bar; I mean the smell of a lascivious woman. His behavior shows that he is fond of lascivious women, but he has no guts. Even if Little Chen has taken a fancy to another woman, I'm sure she is not a bar girl. That's the last thing for an official to do. As a popular saying goes, 'If a woman is not lascivious, no man will love her.' In order to win over your husband, try to become sexier than his lover."

An'an grinned broadly.

Xiaomin said, "If you catch a big fish this time, you might as well get divorced. Since Little Chen took the initiative to dump you, no one will blame you for profiting from adversity. This will be a new beginning for you."

Tears suddenly welled up in An'an's eyes. She said, "A woman like me has to endure humiliation and suffer indignity in order to recapture her own husband. It's practically sinful for you to make fun of a poor woman like me."

Xiaomin was intimidated into comforting An'an. She toned it down and helped An'an throw away the empty ice cream package.

Xiaomin said, "We will adopt a tactic of luring the enemy in deep. As soon as he discovers this whole new world, he will chase after you fervently.

"Do you think he will chase after me again?"

"Of course." Xiaomin pointed to the street corner, saying, "Here we are."

In the quiet and dark bar the candles on the tables were not lit. It was still early and Shanghai's night life had not started yet. It was the first time An'an had visited a bar. Standing in the center of the bar, she was glancing around. Xiaomin skillfully turned over the chairs on the table and arranged them in order around the table. Her exaggerated actions were usual for those who want to show their own life to their near and dear. Xiaomin wanted to show that she was in her element in her chosen career.

An'an sniffed deeply, saying, "I see the strange smell of your hair actually came from here. No wonder you go to the hospital early in the morning to take a bath. What kind of smell is this?"

Xiaomin said, "It's a mixture of alcohol, cigarette smoke and men's perfume."

An'an sat on a high stool and watched Xiaomin cleaning every wine glass.

"Is that the smell of a lascivious woman?"

The clean wine glasses were sparkling in the lamplight like Xiaomin's necklace made of artificial diamonds. An'an glanced at Xiaomin's necklace. She wanted to have a discussion with Xiaomin, but she couldn't really focus. It was her first visit to a bar. Dressed up like this and seated in a dark background with only one overhead lamp on, she felt like she was in a dream.

Busy cleaning the wine glasses, Xiaomin stole a glance at An'an. She grinned broadly and said, "You do look like one of them. Soon you'll see those unfaithful women. After ten o'clock those women will appear here, but they always sit in dark corners like rats."

An'an bent her head to look at herself and was amused by her own attire. Suddenly she became worried, saying, "I'm afraid of sitting alone in a dark corner."

Xiaomin said, "You don't have to sit at a corner. Please rest assured that there are plenty of bar girls here. If our customers are interested in them, they will negotiate a price. We aren't in the countryside; no one is snatching girls by force."

"What shall I do when Mr. Shi comes? I don't want to play gooseberry."

"You don't need to stay away. Just order the best drinks and snacks you like and let him pay the bill."

An'an uttered a sound of acknowledgment.

Xiaomin saw her raising her head and looking at the customers' business cards stuck on the wall.

She noticed An'an crossing herself unconsciously. It was An'an's habit to cross herself when she was nervous. Xiaomin said, "If Little Chen is a man of conscience, he ought to remember how you fell out with your mother in order to marry him. As a daughter of a well-off family, you had to be reconciled to living with him in the countryside for three years. It was not easy for you to get a house and move back to Shanghai."

An'an said, "You'd better not bring up this subject. I'm so furious that I may spit blood. When I seized the household registry booklet to go ahead with my marriage registration, my mom said, the day will come when you cry for help. She also said, when that day comes, don't eat your words and come back to my home. As I've made my bed, now I have to lie on it. Don't you think so?"

"It's not that serious. You talk as if it were the tragic story of Liang Shanbo and Zhu Yingtai in traditional Chinese opera," Xiaomin shook her head.

An'an took no heed of her comforting words and said, "Sometimes, when I think about the whole thing, I really want to curse."

"Just swear loudly. What are you afraid of?" said Xiaomin.

"What swear word shall I use?" An'an was wringing her hands on the table. "I'd like to use the strongest swear word."

Xiaomin said, "What about 'fuck your mom'?"

An'an grinned broadly, saying, "OK."

She was laughing. She opened her mouth, but not a sound was uttered.

"Go ahead! There's nobody here," said Xiaomin.

After a brief hesitation, An'an remained silent with her mouth open.

Xiaomin said, "I'll teach you how a foreigner uses a swear word. I learned from an English sailor. You just say 'fuck you.'"

"What does it mean?" asked An'an. She still tried to use the previous swear word.

"The same as the Chinese swear word 'fuck your mom.'"

"Fuck you!" An'an swore under her breath.

Then An'an swore loudly, "Fuck you! Fuck you!"

An'an kept Xiaomin company the whole evening. She behaved like a curious and shy girl. Mr. Shi brought his tall cousin to the bar. Xiaomin had a better opinion of his cousin than of Mr. Shi. His cousin was wearing a short-sleeved T-shirt. His tanned arms were revealed in the lamplight and his skin looked delicate and soft. Xiaomin guessed that he must have been to a sauna. She felt she was about to achieve her aspirations after such a long wait. Her Mr. Right finally appeared in front of her. It was surely the hand of fate. She was so overwhelmed by her sentiment that her eyes were alight and she was full of witty remarks. Her unusual excitement drew Linda's attention. She came past the counter and winked broadly at Xiaomin.

Mr. Shi's cousin remained calm and composed. He was neither talkative nor apathetic. When he found An'an ill at ease, he took the initiative to talk with her. Blushing like a virgin, An'an was not as bold and forthcoming as Xiaomin.

When they parted, it was late at night. Usually

Xiaomin worked until midnight, but that day Xiaomin and An'an left in the small hours of the morning. It was Mr. Shi's cousin who saw An'an sitting unsteadily on the stool because of her sleepiness. While patting An'an on the arm, he said to Xiaomin, "This one is like a child who can sleep in a seated position. Go and bring her back home. We can't bear to see her so sleepy."

Xiaomin brought An'an outside to a lamp post. As there was no bus service, she called a taxi for her. After she saw An'an almost fall into the taxi, she gave the money to the driver and said to An'an, "I've paid the fare."

An'an said from inside, "I'll pay for taxi myself."

Then she poked her head out of the window. In the lamplight Xiaomin saw two blushing spots on An'an's face. Xiaomin rushed over and gave An'an a quick hug. She was soft and fragrant. Xiaomin said, "I do hope you two will be reconciled. I work until midnight every day for the sole purpose of giving myself a decent home."

A few days later, back at the bar, Xiaomin's small

white and nimble hand pushed a can of beer across the counter to Mr. Shi under the lamplight.

"You're alone today. Where's your cousin?" asked Xiaomin.

"He's interested in a piece of land in Qingpu. He's gone there to inspect the land. He's planned to set up a factory."

"What's the benefit of opening a factory in the countryside? At night there's not a single soul to be seen. If he goes ahead with his plan, I'm afraid he won't be free even at night."

"Miss, you do care for him? As an old saying goes, 'From ancient times to the present all the beauties love handsome young men.' Now that I'm an old man, no girl will take heed of me even if I'm fairly rich."

"Since we're old friends, why should you feel jealousy? I will always care for you. As a rich businessman, too many girls will show concern for you."

"I'm absolutely fed up with the life here. Just like Taiwan 20 years ago, the streets are congested with traffic and people are becoming increasingly voracious. It always gives me a bad headache. When

I go back home at night, I only have my shadow to keep me company. I really don't know how to tie-over those monotonous days." Mr. Shi shook his head.

Xiaomin said, "You're far from being a miserable wretch. You have numerous concubines, and you enjoy yourself immensely."

Mr. Shi took out a long jewel box from his pocket and laid it on Xiaomin's hand, saying, "I took this from my own shop and will present it to my concubine. The necklace I gave you last time and this wrist chain combine to make a set. The Czech diamonds are world-famous."

Xiaomin opened the small box and took out a diamond wrist chain. The sparkling wrist chain made Xiaomin's eyes shine. Xiaomin put it on and admired its elegance. Then she said to Mr. Shi, "Go and have your drink. Don't stare at me blankly. Your expression is frightening me."

Mr. Shi filled about half of the glass. There was no more beer coming out of the can. He shook the can and a cracking sound could be heard. But he still failed to pour the beer out. Xiaomin took the can over and shook it. Then she pressed her eyes near the opening of the pop-top beer can and looked inside. She cracked a smile and handed it back to Mr. Shi, saying, "You're destined to get this beer can."

Mr. Shi took it over and looked inside, too. As it was put in the fridge for a fairly long time, some of the beer was frozen.

"Miss, you're a very calculating girl. You deliberately selected this can as a return gift. I know you want me to think of a way to get the beer out." With these words he wiped the can clean and put it in the crotch between his legs. He said, "It will melt the fastest here."

Xiaomin could not help laughing and covered her mouth with her hand. She said, "You're very smart indeed." Mr. Shi said, "Don't forget the ring. Show me how you look when you have the ring on."

With a smile, Xiaomin took the diamond ring from the box. She took off her butterfly-shaped ring and put on the new ring.

The doorbell rang as the door opened and Linda called out, "Are you alone, Mister?"

Xiaomin cast a glance in that direction. The new-comer was none other than Little Chen, who was dressed in a white suit. He let his eyes roam round the bar. It was clear that he had come to meet her.

Looking over Mr. Shi's shoulder, which was as fragrant and soft as fresh bread, Xiaomin saw Little Chen's face hidden in the dark and flickering candlelight. He looked like a stray cat mewing outside the window at night.

With a smile, Xiaomin looked at Mr. Shi in the lamplight and saw his eyes glowing with delight. She waved her hand in front of his eyes, saying, "I told you not to stare at me like this. You look like an old wolf."

"Old wolf?" Mr. Shi still focused his eyes on her. "I'm afraid one word is missing. In the mainland, children start their schoolwork by writing simplified Chinese characters. Tonight, you went so far as to skip an important word. I'll make you drink wine as a forfeit."

Xiaomin burst into laughter. She said, "What word did I skip?"

"You skipped the word 'seductive' to save my face."

Xiaomin shook her head with a smile, saying, "I didn't say you're a seductive old wolf. That's your own opinion."

Mr. Shi drank his beer and smiled, "Yes, that's my own opinion. Miss, you're clever at playing tricks. You would be wasting your talents even if you worked as my secretary."

Little Chen's face looked like a small strip of dry and hard bok choy which had shrunken in the fridge. When Xiaomin's eyes and Little Chen's eyes locked together, Xiaomin covered her eyes with her hand and rubbed her eyes, saying loudly, "That Japanese is smoking his cigar again. The cigar smoke is so irritating that I can't open my eyes."

"Shall I help you rub your eyes?" Mr. Shi reached out his fat hand and placed it on her face. Xiaomin intended to whisk it away and then changed her mind. Mr. Shi's hand touched her nose and she could smell the perfume in his fingers. She felt his fingers were as soft as those of an old lady. She thought of his cousin. She was sure his cousin's fingers were not as senile as his.

She heard Linda greeting Little Chen. When you closed your eyes, you could sense Linda's voice was so sexy that it lured him to the dark corner. So long as Little Chen was fascinated by Linda, she herself would be released.

At the thought of this, she opened her eyes and pushed Mr. Shi's hand away. She recoiled a little and said in a half smiling manner, "People like you are always flirting with us."

When she glanced around, she saw Linda standing under a lamp and smiling at her. She said, "Meibo, you're very lucky in love tonight. There's a gentleman there who asked for you to meet him."

When she walked out from behind the counter, Xiaomin was itching to kill him. However, she still poured a glass of beer and brought it to him. On the way she imagined that the beer was poisoned wine, a knife or a gun and she was not herself but An'an. It might be safer. She came to Little Chen's table and pushed the glass of beer toward him. Leaning on the back of the chair, she was staring at him without saying a word.

"Is that bald man your boyfriend?" asked Little Chen.

"It's none of your business," said Xiaomin.

"It seems to me that he's kept you as a mistress. If you like to be kept by him, I'll give up, because I'm not rich enough to be his rival. But why did you use An'an as an excuse? You act like a whore who is eager to have a chastity arch built for her."

"It's none of your business," said Xiaomin.

"Please answer my question why do you want to dump me? If you tell me the truth, I will never disturb you again."

"You've no money. It's not because I look down upon you, but because, as you admitted just now, you're not rich enough to be his rival. I don't necessarily want him, but I'm certain I don't want you. Well, I've stated my reasons. Are you happy about an open quarrel?"

"I wonder why girls today have no sense of shame."

"Then you should ask yourself why men of your kind fail to win the heart of young girls. All good-looking girls go abroad. I don't think this does you men credit. A man's virtue lies in taking a proper measure of himself."

After uttering these remarks, Xiaomin saw Little Chen open his mouth. She shook her hand hurriedly, saying, "Come on, what's the use of arguing? I've got to go. Since you're already here, enjoy yourself for the time being. But don't take liberties with those bar girls. They will charge you for their service."

When Xiaomin walked away from Little Chen's table, Linda appeared out of the darkness like a ghost. She flashed Xiaomin a smile. Xiaomin gave her a light tap, saying, "Why are you all smiles? He's your patron."

Xiaomin went back to her counter and chatted with Mr. Shi in a rambling way.

She did not see Little Chen anymore. When Mr. Shi left for home at midnight, she walked him to the door. She noticed Little Chen's table was empty except his glass of beer—still full.

8

The next day when she got to her workplace, Xiaomin found her colleagues glancing at her with strange expressions. On her way to her office she walked past a line of cedars which didn't turn green—even in summer. People looked at her cautiously yet excitedly;

pity accompanied by weak smiles. To Xiaomin's mind, their strange expressions were just their efforts to cover up their pleasure in her misfortune. Their sense of public morality forbade them from sneering at her, at the loser, but their nature made them gloat over the loser's misfortune. They wanted to get the inside story, but equally didn't want to seem like country bumpkins. As a result, they feigned a cautious and composed attitude. Since she moonlighted as a barmaid, Xiaomin had a guilty conscience. Naturally she thought she had finally been found out. Xiaomin did not want to lose her present job because of this. She liked to play safe. That's why she went to great pains to greet the colleagues she used to despise and hoped that they might exchange pleasantries. However, they only cast a curious look at her and said a few meaningless words.

Pondering this on her way to the office, Xiaomin felt sure that her forced smile made her look deceptive and guilty.

The minute she entered her office, her colleague said the administrative office of the hospital had called and asked her to go there immediately. Xiaomin turned about and pretended to change clothes so that her shrewd colleague might not notice her panic. She fixed her eyes on a piece of paper stuck on the wall corner and it looked like a urinalysis report. Though muddle-headed, she still asked herself at heart why this urinalysis report came to her office. She was surprised by her own mental clarity. In the heat of the moment she was still able to focus on this report. She braced herself and attempted her best "devil-may-care" sort of attitude.

Casually, she asked, "What is so urgent?"

Her colleague told her it was about An'an.

Xiaomin was stunned. She did not expect that something would have happened with An'an. Little Chen must have been so humiliated by her remarks that after he left the bar in a state, and in order to get back at her, he took the risk of mutual destruction and tried to get her to react by revealing everything to An'an. Although she was An'an's confidante, Xiaomin had pulled the rug out from under her. An'an would never let go of her now. This time Xiaomin thought she herself was done for.

Her colleague asked, "How is Little Chen

capable of that?"

Xiaomin was at a loss for words.

Her colleague said, "An'an is pretty useless. How could she make this kind of thing public in the hospital? She showed no consideration for her own dignity. When she called, it wasn't yet office hours. The switchboard operator on night duty was Little Yu. It's known to all she has a loose tongue. An'an even asked her to pass on the message to the head of the administration office. How stupid she was!" Xiaomin thought ... An'an is well aware that Little Yu is fond of gossip. When they called each other in the hospital, An'an often reminded her that Little Yu was on duty and they should be discreet. An'an was not stupid. She resorted to this on purpose, to defame Xiaomin. Xiaomin realized that An'an had finally declared war on her.

Her colleague still asked, "How come she didn't tell you first? You two are such good friends."

Xiaomin was clever enough to know the implications of these words. She turned around to button up. She said, "I don't have a telephone at home."

Her colleague nodded her head, saying, "Of course, I forgot, what a poor memory I have!"

Xiaomin asked brazenly, "What happened to Little Chen?"

Her colleague said, An'an called early in the morning to say that Little Chen did not come back home last night. She feared that some accident might have happened to him, so she went to the police station and reported it to the police. When she returned home, she was informed that Little Chen was arrested by the police while sleeping with a prostitute at a hotel. It so happened that the police of Jing'an District launched a campaign to crack down on crime last night. He was caught red-handed and was being held in custody at the police station.

Xiaomin stared at her colleague and saw only the plucked curved eyebrows on her face. Her eyebrows looked like the coiled dead earthworms she used to see in her childhood. She remained silent.

She suddenly recalled that Linda was nowhere to be found after Little Chen disappeared last night.

Her colleague said, "I was told that An'an cried bitterly on the phone. It's a terrible misfortune."

Right then the phone began ringing again. The administration office inquired whether Xiaomin had arrived. A woman cadre from the administration office and Xiaomin went to An'an's home together. The cadre told Xiaomin that An'an said on the phone that she was too ashamed to show her face. Since An'an was a petite and delicate girl, the hospital authorities were afraid that she might take things too hard.

By this time Xiaomin had started to straighten out her thoughts. She was relieved that so far she had not been involved. But she had a sense of guilt. If it had not been for her behavior, An'an and Little Chen would not have broken up. She also regretted having hurt Little Chen with those unfeeling remarks. If she had exercised some restraint and persuaded Little Chen to give up his stubborn idea, he would not have gone to bed with Linda. Tormented by both a guilty conscience and profound regret, she despised Little Chen all the more. She did not expect that Little Chen was such a loser, and she never liked an unfortunate man.

As Xiaomin walked through the hospital on her way to the administration office, she did not care anymore about her colleagues' curious looks. An'an's incident was simply a piece of social news which had excited them. They were delighted to hear the strange, but not so serious news. Xiaomin thought about how excited they would have been if they had learned about their love triangle!

She stopped talking about An'an's incident. With a grim expression she climbed the stairs. She thought it was the appropriate expression to wear as An'an's best friend.

They came to An'an's home. Several weeks had passed since Xiaomin climbed up the same stairs the last time. The renovation of the house downstairs was finished. The door and windows were no longer open. Even the window of the kitchen was covered with a white Venetian blind to protect privacy. While walking up the stairs, Xiaomin recalled the days when she hurried up those same stairs and jumped into Little Chen's big bed anxiously. That seemed a lifetime ago.

An'an had such anxiety that her mouth grew a big boil overnight. Holding the doorframe, she broke down in tears.

There behind An'an were the gaily-colored curtains Xiaomin had bought. They were drawn apart in an orderly way. The whole room was bathed in sweltering summer sunshine. The first impression the room gave was a jubilant atmosphere.

The whole day An'an only uttered one remark, "I don't know how to go forward with my life."

As soon as Little Chen was released from custody, An'an filed for divorce. In the beginning their employers tried to dissuade her from applying for a divorce. An'an said to them, "If your husband sleeps with a prostitute, do you still allow him to get into your bed?" This argument silenced them at once.

When they put themselves in her place, they gave up the idea of persuasion.

During that period An'an became emaciated. When she was wearing a blue operating gown, her thin and small body seemed so light that it could be blown away by a gust of wind. When she bought her lunch, the cook would give her an extra portion of gravy to express his sympathy for her. When some young doctors showed compassion and concern for her, An'an always asked Xiaomin to keep her company. She would never give a male doctor the chance to meet her alone. Sometimes Xiaomin was forced to say, "I don't want to play gooseberry."

An'an said, "Please do me a favor and save me from their attention."

Xiaomin said, "But they're good men."

An'an said, "Why don't you find your Mr. Right among them?"

"I am not interested in them because they're poor. That's a simple answer." At the thought of this, Xiaomin praised An'an, "So you finally came round to the logical idea. When you don't take your misfortune to heart, try to moonlight at a high-class bar. You may find an ideal and rich life companion there. As an old saying goes, misfortune may be an actual blessing."

Right there and then An'an cast a sad glance at her as if she were an abandoned wife in a sentimental novel.

She said, "I'm in no state of mind for a job in that kind of place."

During that time, Xiaomin did play the role of An'an's confidante. Every night An'an would call

Xiaomin at the bar. Xiaomin would chat with her patiently. Only when Mr. Shi and his cousin came in would Xiaomin hang up the phone to entertain them.

She told them about An'an's incident.

She told them the story to prove to them that a man is often the cause of a woman's misfortune. While telling the story, she stole glances at them from time to time. Usually, she acted like the owner of the bar instead of one of the frivolous bar girls. But her warmth and sympathy was accompanied by an occasionally bellicose temperament. In the twinkling of an eye, she could turn against a friend without mercy. However, when she met somebody she actually took a fancy to, she was at a loss. As a result, she would resort to behaving like a bar girl. In her mind, this constituted flirting with a member of the opposite sex.

Xiaomin had to admit she didn't see herself as a thoroughly modern woman because she really was at a loss in figuring out how to deal with a man she found attractive. She was surprised at her own conclusion. She had always imagined herself a good example of the various suggestions and admonitions she made to other women. Sometimes she deliberately reached her hand across the counter to pat Mr. Shi's cousin on the arm in order to conceal her bashfulness.

That night when An'an called the bar again, the boss was so infuriated that he said to Xiaomin in a mocking tone, "We'll set up a hotline at the bar and you'll take charge of it." Xiaomin tried to explain to her boss what had happened. The boss told Xiaomin that if her friend's life was too dull, she was always welcome to come to the bar. He said, "Some of our customers like this kind of sentimental story. She may find her alter ego here." The boss generously said, "Since she's your friend, I won't charge her for drinks in the beginning. When she becomes a regular bar girl, we'll have a further discussion. Am I generous enough?"

Xiaomin called An'an immediately to urge her to accept the boss's offer. An'an said on the phone, "How can a fallen woman work in such a place?"

"Well, don't deflate your own morale," Xiaomin comforted her. "Come here. Some customers take a special fancy to pathetic beauties like you. You're a flower still wet with dew. Come here at once."

Just then Mr. Shi and his cousin appeared. Mr. Shi had really taken a fancy to Xiaomin, but Xiaomin had a crush on his cousin. If Mr. Shi did not come, his cousin never seemed to come alone. It seemed to her that he didn't know how to flirt with a woman. Xiaomin thought that this was a fairly reliable man and that she needed to move not to miss her chance. She must prevent Mr. Shi from slipping away until his cousin was willing to come to the bar by himself.

A moment later, An'an arrived. Standing in the lamplight, she was wearing a dress with brightly colored pattern which they had seen while window-shopping at the Bund, and a pair of white leather shoes. Xiaomin examined An'an's figure. She was certain An'an was wearing the bra which they purchased together in order to tantalize Little Chen. With this little help, she looked very well-proportioned. Her mature and graceful body complemented by her sad and lonely expression made her look like a Hollywood star of the 1930s.

Mr. Shi was the first to react to her arrival. Sitting on the high stool, he opened his short arms, saying, "Here is our sad beauty."

Looking at them, An'an tried to crack a smile, but she was on the verge of tears.

Acting like her guardian angel, Mr. Shi's cousin went over to support An'an's elbow, saying, "Let her calm down first."

He showed An'an to a small table and pulled out the chair for her.

The dark room looked like a river. The red candles Xiaomin lit at the beginning of her shift looked like lotus flowers on the river. The flickering light of the candle brightened a small patch of the table. Xiaomin followed them with her eyes. Before sitting down, An'an cast a glance at her. The gentle and charming look on her beautiful and fair face told Xiaomin all she wanted to know. Mr. Shi's cousin obviously adored her.

Pretty soon a white Mercedes Benz was waiting to pick her up when An'an got off work. Xiaomin pretended to know nothing about it. She never asked An'an any questions or kept her company when going back home. In this way she tried to avoid experiencing her disappointment directly. An'an did not mention this. Nor did she ask Xiaomin to keep her company after getting off work. They acted as if they had never kept each other company before. They never talked about what had happened at the bar. Their relationship cooled down without open hostility.

Xiaomin worked at the bar every night. Mr. Shi went back to Taiwan. No regular customers talked with her all the time anymore. Late at night she often rested her chin on her hands and recalled what had happened in the past summer. It seemed like a dream to her. She pondered hard and tried to fathom its meaning. She failed to interpret its meaning, but she could not forget it completely. The dream was hidden deep in her heart. But it flashed across her mind from time to time.

On a Sunday soon thereafter, her parents went to visit Grandma. Xiaomin went too. She got up late that morning. When she reached Grandma's home, her mother was sitting in a small living room partitioned by Grandma with a sofa. Her mother was seated in front of the floor lamp. Xiaomin had bought a similar one for An'an's new home. It seemed to Xiaomin that a new maid had come to Grandma's home.

Her mother probably guessed what Xiaomin was thinking. She never smiled at Xiaomin first. She only smiled back when she saw Xiaomin smiling at her. As far as Xiaomin could remember, her mother had never held her in her arms.

Her mother told Grandma she was not used to Shanghai's prosperity. She felt dizzy when she strolled in this dazzling metropolis.

In Xiaomin's eyes, her mom acknowledged her own inferiority while Grandma still regarded the new prosperity of Shanghai as unworthy of notice. She realized there was an unbridgeable gap between herself and both of them. They lacked common language in every respect. She sat to one side, lost in thought. As she sat near the bathroom door, she could see through to the wet laundry Grandma had left hanging over the bathtub. To the best of her memory, it was Grandma's usual practice to air-dry her wet laundry in the bathroom. According to Grandma's principle, high-quality clothing would be damaged by the sunshine whereas the low-quality clothing hung on the balcony would reveal your shabbiness. In fact, Xiaomin did not like to worry too much about face-saving like Grandma. She had high aspirations and wanted to live an affluent life. Though Grandma's past appealed to her enormously, she had a desire to live more happily than her grandmother did now.

She knew very well this age belonged to her. It was the harsh reality her mother and grandmother had to face, even if it made one of them dizzy and the other cursed it for being both a sham and obscene. She really felt she needed to seize this golden opportunity and achieve her goal of living an affluent life.

In her imagination, if Grandma had been born 60 years later, she would have been driven by insatiable desires. If her mom had been born 30 years later, she would have been as gentle and charming as An'an. A simple-minded woman who might have had a happy lot.

An'an was an interesting case. If Little Chen had not taken a fancy to her and quarreled fiercely with An'an, An'an would not have divorced him and found a sugar daddy. Her comfortable life now went way beyond her previous expectations.

If Little Chen had not chosen her instead of An'an, An'an would not have come to the bar and met Mr. Shi's cousin. It might be Xiaomin herself who sat in a Mercedes.

If An'an had not gone to the countryside, she would not have had an affair with Little Chen. They had known each other for several years, and they had never had any illicit relations before then.

If it had not been for her sake, Little Chen would not have come to such a place. He would not have had the guts to sleep with Linda at a hotel. Then An'an would not have had the reason to divorce him.

If she had not constantly seen during her childhood how Grandma eked out a living with daily attention and caution, she would not have set such a personal goal when she was a child.

Lost in a myriad of thoughts, she concluded that she had lousy luck this year and thanks to her, her close friends were down on their luck, too. But deep at heart she was aware that bad luck was only an excuse. In fact, she must have been punished by Heaven for committing a terrible wrong.

She was an egocentric Shanghai girl who would fight for her interests. But her guidelines were simply to benefit herself without harming others. Of course, her primary concern was to benefit herself, not inflicting harm on others was of secondary importance. She was deeply upset by the fact that she inadvertently harmed herself at others' expense.

One day, during rush hour when everyone got off work, and the streets were busy with a constant stream of people and vehicles, Xiaomin walked alone on her way back home and somebody bumped into her. It was only too natural for people to bump against each other in the crowded streets in Shanghai. Xiaomin did not mind. She kept on walking. As the summer season was approaching its end, Shanghai was frequently visited by typhoons. With a recent typhoon passing away, the street was dotted with pools of dark rainwater. Intuitively, people veered toward the fairly dry parts of the street. Xiaomin had earphones on and listened to a music program of the radio station. As she turned up the volume, her ears were filled with Wang Jingwen's song: "I'm really willing / I'm really willing / I'm really willing." Xiaomin's mind overflowed with her thrilling voice. Xiaomin thought, I'm really willing, but what I'm willing to do is far, far away from reality. A pathetic feeling came over her.

Right there and then, somebody bumped her from behind. She turned her head and was about to say "Watch your step!" when she found it was Little Chen.

Little Chen's hair was wet. He looked like pickled vegetables—poor, wet and rumpled. It had actually been difficult for Xiaomin to recognize him. His appearance raised goose bumps on her arms.

"What do you want?"

"I demand compensation. You've ruined my future and my family. I have nothing left. I demand compensation," said Little Chen. Hearing his remarks, Xiaomin thought she was dreaming.

"What? Are you crazy?" said Xiaomin.

"I demand compensation," said Little Chen.

"That's because you and that bar girl got into hot water. Your behavior was really disgusting!" Xiaomin freed her sleeve from the grip of his dirty-nailed hand and smoothed it gently with her hand.

"It's because of you. Without you, ours was a happy family. Your arrival ruined our family. You have to pay back for my losses."

The passers-by cast an inquisitive glance at them. A flush of embarrassment rose to her cheeks.

It so happened that a red taxi came to a stop by her side. She saw a hand passing on the money to the driver over the dirty organic glass shield. Xiaomin fixed her eyes on Little Chen and said with a sneer, "How shall I compensate you?"

"You'll get married with me," Little Chen said without batting an eyelid.

Xiaomin got so worked up that she burst into laughter.

The door of the taxi opened and a woman with a child came out. Xiaomin rushed into the car before the door closed and left Little Chen behind on the sidewalk. She said to the driver, "I'm catching a plane. Please hurry up."

Xiaomin had simply dumped Little Chen. It was like a scene in a movie. Unfortunately, she did not live in a movie. She had to go to work every day.

Little Chen was transferred to a factory. When the factory planned to lay off workers, Little Chen was in the first batch to be fired. The employer gave a somewhat plausible reason: As a capable man, Little Chen could benefit by earning big money. As a laid-off worker, Little Chen idled away his life. That's why he intercepted her in the street. He said he had let An'an down and he wished her all the best. As he had to live his own life, he wanted Xiaomin to keep him company. He was not so broad-minded as to heartily wish that Xiaomin would find a well-off businessman and lead a happy life while he himself lived a miserable life.

He saw himself as the most reasonable man on earth. He would return good for good and evil for evil.

Little Chen waited for Xiaomin under every tree and at every intersection.

In her heart Xiaomin had intended to kill Little Chen thousands of times. She tried her best to avoid disclosure of the secret. With An'an's divorce from Little Chen, it was natural for her to think that their affair would not pose a threat to her anymore. If this secret of hers was made public now, she would make herself a laughingstock. Even An'an would laugh at her with her colleagues. Xiaomin recalled the offhand remark An'an had uttered, "It's time for a clever woman like you to retire!"

That day Little Chen came to harass her again.

Xiaomin could not bear it anymore and gave him a push.

He had stood on the curb. With Xiaomin's sudden push, he fell down on the street. The screeching of brakes could be heard in the congested street. Xiaomin thought he had been run over. But an instant later she saw him standing up slowly amid an endless stream of bikes.

Xiaomin happened to see a white Mercedes moving slowly by on the other side of the curb. Little Chen fell down and was buffered by the car. Little Chen did not notice it, but Xiaomin saw the side window rising slowly beside the driver's seat. Before the window blocked her view, she caught sight of An'an in the car.

Her beautiful face looked nice before, but it had acquired a gorgeous look now. The diamond earrings on her ears sparkled, the brilliant light of the diamonds illuminating her smiling face. Though her smile was faint, her glowing face looked like a burning briquette which radiates happiness without a flame.

Xiaomin could not believe her eyes. With the tinted window tightly shut, her former confidante drove her Mercedes slowly past Little Chen, who was still standing on the street, and then she sped by.

In Memory of the Departed

Shanghai: the summer of 1944. Although the French had already relinquished their long-held Shanghai Concession in the gunfire of the Pacific War, the roadside sycamores planted under the French municipal development plans were still growing, and overhung the length and breadth of one street after another. That section of the city of Shanghai, with its glamorous stores as well as secluded neighborhoods, still boasted high real estate value. The European-style houses with their gardens spoke of a life of comfort. Thanks to the excellent drainage system, moisture on the road surface here dried up more quickly than in other parts of the city. Bakeries, photo studios, pharmacies, ballet schools and beauty salons run by Russian émigrés, Jewish-owned jewelry shops, shoe stores, fur shops, restaurants, and German medical clinics remained attractive to those who embraced Western styles of living, especially to some of the new arrivals to the city. The Pacific War was drawing to an end, but no one knew that at the time. As the war dragged on year after year, many people in Shanghai managed to get on with their lives as usual amid the chaos. Children born and raised in wartime took their life to be the way it was supposed to be. That August, *Shen Bao* (*The Shanghai News*) even carried advertisements for a new coffee shop and the Huiluo Company's big annual sale.

"But you must not be misled by appearances," said an old citizen of Shanghai to me. "After the Commercial Press was destroyed in the Japanese air-raids of Baoshan and the Shanghai East Library was burned to the ground, life in Shanghai was never the same again." On the day of the Baoshan air-raids, ashes from the burning East Library were blown into the city proper like flakes of snow and blocked out the sun and the sky for a whole day. "Life in Shanghai at that time," continued the elderly man, "was by no means as peaceful as it appeared to be."

In August of that summer, a baby girl was born in a foreign-owned women's hospital. The Western-trained obstetrician cut the umbilical cord with a pair of sterilized scissors, tied it up, and wrapped it in sterilized gauze. A nurse took over the baby girl's care before she had even opened her eyes.

The baby's mother was movie star Shangguan Yunzhu.

Shangguan Yunzhu was a petite woman from a small town in the lower reaches of the Yangtze River. She was an exquisite beauty with delicate facial features typical of women of that region. She had come to Shanghai at age 18 with other war refugees. Like many other non-natives who later rose to prominence in Shanghai, she had come to Shanghai looking for nothing more than a safe haven in a crowded house in a relatively safe foreign Concession. Yet, opportunity, hidden in the ambitious yet modest life of the urban petty bourgeoisie of Shanghai, came to knock at her door.

Like most other women in Shanghai at the time, she needed to work to make a living. It was said that on the very first day of her job as a cashier in Mr. He's Photo Studio next to Cathay Movie Theater, the studio owner took her shopping for stylish clothes, treating her like a delicate flower vase decorating his studio. And on her part, she took this as her first lesson of survival in the glamorous city of Shanghai, a lesson that taught her the importance of appearance for women and marked the beginning of her life-long love affair with clothes.

And so, a few years later, just like any other fairy tale that played out in this city of opportunities, this native of Changjing, who couldn't even speak Mandarin, became a star on the stage as well as on the big screen. Although born with the name Wei Junluo, she now went by the name of Shangguan Yunzhu. She poured her heart into her acting roles. In her ardent hope of making a success of herself in Shanghai's soft-core show biz, she offered herself to her agents by way of repaying them. In order to make herself look prettier on screen, she, like other actresses, regularly gave gifts of fashionable neckties, foreign cigarettes and chocolates to the cameramen, even though they conceded that there was no need for such a beauty to do so. On days when the filming ended early, she went joyfully with colleagues to dance and eat late night snacks. Even the lowly stagehands commented that she had none of the airs of a movie star. When her theatrical company was on tour outside of Shanghai, it was invariably she who socialized with local big shots to make sure that the shows could go on day after day. She was a true professional ready to give her all to her acting career. Once, she lost control of herself while shooting on set, playing a woman in despair, and broke down in wails of grief.

She had very attractive eyebrows and eyes. With her eyebrows plucked thin and arched and her pointed chin resting on the gold-filigree-piped collar of her fitted silk *qipao* dress, she was the very image of a calculating and sophisticated Shanghai beauty. She mixed a hint of coquettishness with the dutifulness of a pretty girl of humble birth. That was why directors often picked her for roles as Shanghai social butterflies, young wives of rich merchants, and imperious wives of the nouveau riche. Under her thin, painted eyebrows, her sprightly eyes could be as chilling as the sharpest razor. The suggestion of a smile hovering about her lips gave expression to a sophisticated, cosmopolitan woman's inner candor. That was why she could play the leading role in Eileen Chang's *Long Live the Mrs*. However, once her makeup was removed and her permed hair combed straight with hair oil, her face would look as innocent and unsophisticated as weeds on a dirt road, and the shadows under her cheekbones told of pain and frayed nerves. One couldn't help wondering if this pretty girl from a backwater small town, with little education and no patron, had some secrets that helped her hold her own in the vanity fair of Shanghai where the strong preyed on the weak. The roles she had played included a raped factory girl, a desperate housemaid with nowhere to go, and other downtrodden women struggling feebly against their doomed fate.

By 1944 she had already achieved stardom, but how many people could truly appreciate her brilliance that shone through the poorly written plays and the snowy screens? Like a diamond perfunctorily laid in a common wooden box, she always dazzled with a light that was out of place with her surroundings. Was she aware that her talent was being wasted by the movies churned out in Shanghai at the time? Was that why she was always desperately on the lookout for opportunities to shine brighter? This ambition of hers was often construed to be motivated by something else, such as a wish to attain the popularity of stars like Hu Die, "Miss Butterfly Wu" (movie queen in the 1930s), or to achieve the extravagant lifestyle of the other screen giants. In a place as flashy as Shanghai, a successful career was always associated with material comforts and vanity with nebulous distinctions between the two.

By then she had also left the humble house where she first settled when she arrived in Shanghai. She had abandoned her first husband and her first son who were still living in a garret, and had married a man with an illustrious name in the theatrical establishments of Shanghai. They set up a home in the upscale Yongkang Villa in the French Concession. Her bathroom faucets had brass cross-handles with porcelain buttons marked H for hot and C for cold. Her spacious wardrobe was filled to spilling with all manner of clothes, *qipao* and matching shawls, purses, embroidered shoes, silk hosiery, and self-made tights and girdles with multiple buttons and knots to keep her waist in shape. Sometimes, before she sent her clothes to the laundry after only one or two wearings, her wardrobe was drenched with the mixed scent of face-powder cakes and fragrant white magnolia buds. Perhaps she had hung over the frog buttons of her *qipao* some fragrant white magnolia buds strung on thin wire in a fan-like row that were sold in the streets.

Flower girls with their shallow bamboo baskets stood on street corners and cried out "White magnolia buds and gardenia!" when they saw well-dressed women approach. Shangguan's exquisite wardrobe, with its blend of aromas, contained all that a Shanghai movie star of 1944 needed for the big screen.

The father of the baby girl was Yao Ke, a dashing young man from Suzhou and a Yale University graduate. With his well-oiled hair showing traces of comb teeth, he sported a white jacket and a pinstriped thin woolen vest, and he peppered his speech with English words. He had brought back an American wife. On the second floor of the French Club next to the French Park, there was a small elegant auditorium where left-leaning Shanghai college students often staged plays in English. Among the audience were members of the underground Communist Party, including Wang Yuanhua and his wife Zhang Ke. Yao Ke often took his American wife there. He was the major contributor and editor of *The T'ien Hsia Monthly*, the only English magazine in China at the time. He was also deeply involved in the translation of Lu Xun's works and spent a great deal of time in Lu Xun's company. After Lu Xun died of illness, a grand funeral was held in the Wanguo Funeral Home. According to the Western custom whereby family members and close friends of the deceased carry the coffin, Lu Xun's coffin was borne by his closest disciples, and Yao Ke was one of the ten pallbearers. Liu Bannong, author of the sentimental song *How Can I not Miss Her*, and a frequent subject of Lu Xun's satire, was also a good friend of Yao Ke's. Another good friend of his, Yin Fu, was a revolutionary writer later executed at Longhua by the Nationalist Party. Being such a sociable member of the Shanghai intelligentsia, Yao Ke felt good about himself and indulged himself all day in what he enjoyed doing. Being neither "red" nor "white," he committed to neither side, nor did either side try to recruit him, because his Western manners had earned him the nickname "debauched young man about town." Feeling wronged, he complained to Huang Zongjiang, who was a stage actor in Shanghai at the time. More than ten years younger than him, Huang patted him on the shoulder the way an older man treats a junior, and said consolingly, "You are no debauched young man about town. No, siree! You are a big-time good young man about town!"

Rather than taking up a college teaching career as most people who had studied abroad did, Yao Ke devoted his time to writing historical plays as well as directing for the Kugan Theatrical Company. His reputation was said to have rivaled that of the famous stage director Huang Zuolin at the time. Under Japanese surveillance, the stage performers of Shanghai were no longer able to act out episodes of contemporary life on stage, but they were unwilling to give up their acting careers, nor would they stoop to being collaborators. Period drama became their only way out. Goodness knows how many performers in those years honed their skills and satisfied their ambitions in period costumes. It was then that Yao Ke wrote his *Grievances in the Qing Palace*, a play that immediately attracted the most famous actors and directors of Shanghai. Shangguan Yunzhu played a palace maid in it, and it was in the rehearsal hall of the Heavenly Wind Theatrical Company that they got to know each other. In 1942, Yao Ke's American wife returned to the U.S. with their child, and Yao Ke married Shangguan Yunzhu in Beijing.

And so the baby girl was born in wartime

Shanghai, a city under curfew, where the air echoed with the shrill sound of sirens.

Born in the midst of such people in such a city, she was like a drop of fresh water that had fallen into a salty sea. Her pet name was *Baobei* (Darling), but it adopted the intonation for the English word "baby," and sounded very much like pigeon English. Later in her life, when her loved ones had all come to grief, like wooden boats capsized and smashed to smithereens by high winds and spouting waves, the shelter of the neighborhood, with its reassuring sycamore trees, in the city that bore witness to her sorrows, was the last comfort in her reach.

When mother and child were ready to leave the hospital, the nurse quit her job and joined the Shangguan household with the baby girl, to be *Baobei*'s wet nurse and the mother's personal maid. Shangguan Yunzhu called her Secretary.

Seven years later, when *Baobei*'s little brother's wet nurse, a villager from Wuxi, joined their household, she also called her *Baobei* in the English intonation, as everyone else did. "*Baobei*, finish the eggs, quick! They'll smell after they get cold, and they'll be even harder to swallow." "*Baobei*, it's time for your piano practice. Mom will check your playing after she comes home." By that time, she was almost old enough to go to elementary school, and she had a formal name: Yao Yao. Wearing her hair in two thin braids, she was a quiet girl, not as vivacious as most girls her age.

As her nurse found out, Yao Yao often kept her eyes downcast, so that no one could read the expression in her eyes. This grew into a lifelong habit, a habit that helped her get through many an awkward moment. Everybody who had laid eyes on her commented that she was not as pretty as her mother. Her eyebrows and eyes drooped as if to hide something that weighed on her mind. When she lowered her eyes, her whole face looked overcast with a shadow. But what sorrows could such a little girl have when she had everything going right for her? She even appeared with her mother in the movie *Wanderings of San Mao the Orphan*, in a white chiffon embroidered dress, with a bow in her hair. When posing for photographs, she always kept her arms hanging obediently at her sides, like a doll.

As was the practice in other educated and rich families in Shanghai, Shangguan Yunzhu engaged a piano teacher for her daughter. Accompanied by her nurse, Yao Yao went to her piano teacher's home once a week for her lessons. Shangguan made strict rules for *Baobei*, so that she could grow into a properly brought-up lady. Whenever she had a moment to spare, Shangguan would check Yao Yao's playing. If she found it unsatisfactory, she would whack the girl's hand with the bamboo ruler that the maidservant used for needlework. When she was really angry, she would even give Yao Yao a mighty slap across the face.

Zhang Xiaoxiao, Yao Yao's childhood friend, recounted, "Her mother kept such a tight hold on her that if she inadvertently slipped and fell when we were playing, she would immediately beg her nurse not to tell her mother about it. Yao Yao was deeply afraid of her mother."

In 1945, while Shangguan Yunzhu was on a tour in the north with the Nanguo Theatrical Company, Yao Ke took up with another rich woman. Upon her return to Shanghai, Shangguan found out about this and immediately filed for divorce. *Baobei* was not yet two at the time and had learned to say "Daddy," but there was no longer a Daddy at home for her to call for.

When Yao Yao was six years old, Shangguan married Cheng Shuyao, manager of the Lyceum Theater (now the Lanxin Theater). The "uncle" who had always left late disappeared, and this very amiable new one with a long, narrow face, an elegant and courteous Beijing accent and a sincere smile, stayed. His Western-style suits hung in Mom's wardrobe, his suitcases were taken into the walk-in closet at the end of the hallway, his razor with its white ivory handle now lay on the rack in the bathroom, his canvas razor-strop now hung on the back of the bathroom door, and, at the front door stood a pair of slippers that belonged exclusively to him. When Yao Yao called him "Dad," he responded with a hearty "Ay!" in the manner of a Northerner.

When she was seven, a little baby brother was born, to the great joy of Mom and Dad. Their friends all came to offer their congratulations. A pair of lamps received as a gift from the famous actress Wu Yin gave Mom inspiration for his name. Later, when more well-wishers came and asked for the boy's name, they were told that it was Dengdeng (lamp). One day, Yao Yao asked, "How come little brother's surname is

Cheng, and mine is Yao? I also want to be a Cheng. From now on, I am Cheng Yaoyao."

Everyone within hearing burst into laughter.

Sure enough, when she enrolled in elementary school, she signed her name Cheng Yaoyao.

Cheng Shuyao expressly went to see Dengdeng's nurse in her room and told her, "Be nice not only to Dengdeng, but also to Yaoyao." Many years later, after most people in our story had passed away, the nurse could still quote Cheng Shuyao, trying hard to reproduce his Beijing accent. "Mr. Cheng was a good man," she added. "A well-educated man who knew right from wrong. He was really nice to Yao Yao. Whenever he came home from work, he would call out '*Baobei*! *Baobei*!' before he even put down his briefcase and took off his coat. They were as close to each other as birth father and daughter. *Baobei* loved acting the spoiled little girl, but only to Mr. Cheng, not to her mother."

Mr. Cheng had grown up in a multigenerational household in a traditional courtyard house in a Beijing *hutong* as the pampered eldest son of a family that had come down in the world. As a young man he used to sport well-oiled hair, a tuxedo with a necktie, white gloves, and a black satin hat tucked under an arm. His refined, dashing air reminded one of Zhang Xueliang (one-time warlord, who had, in the Xi'an Incident of 1936, and with the aid of another general, kidnapped Chiang Kaishek and imprisoned him until he agreed to form a united front with the Communists against the Japanese invasion).

In those days, it was a regular custom for Yenching University students to elect the most spirited and sociable male student and award him the title "Big Clown." Cheng Shuyao won the distinction and was named Big Clown of the Education Department. Even when his family had eaten away their entire fortune and his younger sister, a graduate from Beiman, the best girls' high school in Beijing, had to give up a college education and hire herself out as a tutor, he continued to live it up at Yenching. According to convention, Yenching freshmen were supposed to behave themselves and, in an annual ritual of hazing those who dared to step over the line, the entire student body would pick out the most unruly freshman and have him thrown, fully clothed, into Weiming Lake on campus. And Cheng Shuyao was the host of this event, year after year. One year, a female student was elected to be the victim and, by popular demand, a male student was supposed to go with her into the lake, and that companion turned out to be none other than Cheng Shuyao. With his love of drama, he acted with Sun Daolin, his Yenching schoolmate, in plays staged by the North South Theatrical Company, of which he was the company director. His long face had the refinement of a well-educated man mixed with the cheerfulness, sincerity, innocence and slyness of a little boy. He afforded Yao Yao the childhood joy of frolicking in his lap on many a late afternoon.

One day, when Yao Yao and her nurse were left alone at home, Yao Yao took a photo from her mother's room and showed it to the nurse. Pointing at the man in the photo, she said, "This is my dad, my own dad. He didn't mean to leave me and Mom. He was just tricked by some bad people and did wrong things, so Mom doesn't want him anymore. He still misses me and Mom."

And then, after the nurse had looked at the photo, she took it back and put it where it belonged.

One day, Yao Yao went to the cartoonist Zhang Leping's house on Wuyuan Road to look for her playmate Zhang Xiaoxiao. Since her mother had taken her to act in *Wanderings of San Mao the Orphan* based on Zhang Leping's cartoons, she often went to the Zhang family's house to play with her friend Xiaoxiao and Xiaoxiao's many siblings. In the next-door neighbor's yard stood an orange tree that was weighed down with yellow fruit in late autumn. Upstairs, Mr. Zhang used to bend over a large table drawing cartoons about the misery of children in pre-Liberation years and the happiness of children in the new society. That day, she said that she had a secret to confide in Zhang Xiaoxiao, and so the two of them went upstairs and sat down. She said that her birth father had learned about her tuberculosis and had asked someone to bring her a letter from Hongkong, along with some British Ostrin calcium booster shots, supposedly to cure her condition. But her mother surrendered the package, unopened, to the security office of the movie studio, although thereafter she did begin to force Yao Yao to eat two eggs every day. Yao Yao had no idea where the expensive calcium shots ended up, nor what the letter said.

"Don't tell anyone about this," said she to her little friend.

The year 1952 saw the beginning of the nationwide campaign against embezzlement, corruption, and theft, during which every work unit conducted investigations of its own staff. In the new China, all the former dancing hostesses employed by Paramount Dance Hall in Shanghai had gone on to other lines of work because the dance hall had too few male patrons to stay solvent, and prostitutes were sent in batches to job-training centers. Even coffee shops on Middle Linsen Road (present-day Middle Huaihai Road) were about to become diners because the owners felt that they were out of step with the simple lifestyle advocated by the new society. Everybody had come to believe that in the new society, which was as pure as a new-born baby, embezzlement of state property, extramarital affairs, thievery, dressing oneself in the fashions of the old society, and wearing diamond rings, were all depravities that stank to high heaven. It was in fact a campaign to sanitize the mores of the entire society. The old Shanghai way of life, with its dedicated attention to details of material comfort, was on the way out.

At this time, suspicions arose at the Lyceum Theater against Manager Cheng Shuyao regarding the way he handled the proceeds of a 1949 charity bazaar which had raised funds from the entertainment industry for the army and for disaster-relief. These accusations immediately brought investigators down to the theater to audit the account books. The fact was, during the charity sales, donations were made in cash and in kind, and there were many temporary helpers from everywhere. And every day, bank employees came to help take the money to the banks. Things were indeed quite chaotic. But Cheng Shuyao had been a darling of Yenching University, a rich boy with deep pockets, and when working in a foreign-owned company, had donated his own money to the North South Theatrical Company. So there was no need for him to stoop low for money's sake. The idea of embezzlement had never even crossed his mind, nor had it ever occurred to him that he would be suspected of embezzling money that belonged to the state. His mind was focused on doing great impressive things, to the neglect of nitty-gritty details that might later be used to prove his innocence, which was why he did not keep an itemized account book. And he had never thought he would one day be audited. So now, without knowing what was good for him, he searched his memory and cooked up an account book, in the belief that the auditing was just part of a routine. The account book was found to be fake the moment the inquiry began. He was locked up in the theater immediately and forbidden to go home.

On the bulletin board reporting on the developments of the campaign at the theater, Cheng Shuyao appeared as an "embezzler."

Yao Yao's nurse went every other day to the theater to bring him food and a change of clothes. The clever woman pretended to be illiterate, but every time she visited, she read carefully what was written on the bulletin board and relayed everything to Shangguan Yunzhu upon returning home. If asked in the theater what she was reading, she replied that she was marveling at the perfectly drawn little circles on the board.

Those were trying times for Shangguan Yunzhu as well. Because she had been a movie star in old Shanghai, she was given only the fourth rank when members of the entertainment industry came under evaluation. Since social butterflies had no place in movies of the new China, her razor-sharp glances had outlived their usefulness. What a blow that ranking was to her, who had been working so very hard! But she never uttered a word of complaint. Instead, she tried fervently to be politically progressive, to be among the first in everything. She threw herself into every fund-raising event for disaster-stricken areas and pro bono performances for the troops until she wore herself out and came down with lung disease. During the Rectification Movement in the entertainment industry, she criticized herself, without being told to, for her bourgeois mode of thinking, saying repeatedly that she was attracted to acting only out of vanity and a desire for the luxurious lifestyle of a star. With a role in the revolutionary play *Song of the Red Flag*, she appeared consecutively in every one of the 131 performances. Whenever she had free time, she took Yao Yao to the rehearsal hall of the art troupe of the People's Liberation Army stationed in Shanghai, to watch their rehearsals of *The White-Haired Girl*. After Cheng Shuyao got into trouble, not a day went by without her weeping at home, but when the nurse said her master had been wronged, she would silence her by saying, "The Communist Party never wrongs anyone."

In his confinement, Cheng Shuyao gave in under constant interrogation. In exchange for freedom so that he would no longer be bothered about this, he admitted to having brought raised funds home. He thought that a few hundred US dollars would buy him peace, little knowing that he was to ruin his future through this confession. Shangguan Yunzhu offered the theater 800 US dollars of her own plus two rings by way of reparation. By the time he was allowed to return home, Cheng Shuyao had already been officially denounced as an embezzler. Stripped of his post as manager, he was to spend the next year laboring under surveillance.

He was almost among the first batch of people purged by the new society. Thereafter, he was to lead the life of a criminal released on bail. Without losing any time, Shangguan Yunzhu filed for divorce. She could no longer live with a man who had turned himself into an embezzler and made her offer her own money as reparation for the allegedly stolen money, so that finally she too had come under suspicion. He implicated her while she was trying so very hard to be accepted, and she had come by her money through honest work, too. When a man besmirches his own name either out of vanity, or snobbishness, or a sense of personal injustice, he stops being clean. In Cheng's case this was partially due to weakness and naivety. But his was a mistake that Shangguan Yunzhu was not going to tolerate.

It was a much publicized divorce, with a resentful Shangguan Yunzhu bursting into torrents of verbal abuse. She should have known the truth of the matter better than anyone else. If her husband had indeed been guilty, he should have hauled home large sacks of money, but she had never laid eyes upon that kind of money. Cheng Shuyao's stupid lie sealed his fate overnight. Left with nothing but self-reproach, he sought compromise in everything, but his submissiveness backfired and further fueled Shangguan's hatred and contempt for him.

All of their acquaintances tried to make peace between them. The nurse did the same, until Shangguan Yunzhu pointed an accusing finger at her and said, "Are you with me or with him?"

Even Cheng Shuming, Cheng Shuyao's younger brother who had just graduated from Tsinghua University and was in Shanghai on a job hunt, tried to act as peacemaker. Taking advantage of his presence, Cheng Shuyao desperately pleaded to Shangguan to keep the family together for the sake of Dengdeng who was not yet two years old. Losing her temper at this supposedly tough Northerner taking refuge behind a little boy, Shangguan Yunzhu gave her husband a slap across the face. At this point, Cheng Shuming stood up and left before he had even had a chance to speak up.

Soon thereafter, on a trip to Beijing for a conference, Shangguan Yunzhu met He Lu, with whom she had been very close before she was married the second time, and they became lovers. After she returned home from Beijing, she stopped nagging Cheng Shuyao for a divorce. Instead, she slumped into melancholy. Quarrels and recriminations stopped, but the atmosphere at home became suffocating and tense. As He Lu kept showing up in Cheng Shuyao's absence, the maidservant and the nurse figured out what was afoot. Upon coming home, Cheng Shuyao would see his wife and He Lu deep in conversation, but they would stop as soon as they saw him. He Lu had been a frequent visitor at the apartment but now looked ill at ease at the sight of Cheng Shuyao. The nurse, who was all for preserving the family for the sake of Dengdeng and Yao Yao, angrily called He Lu a monkey. At long last, on a summer night, husband and wife had a showdown and put an end to the marriage. Both dissolved in tears.

Just as Yao Yao had experienced her mother's divorce at age two, now Dengdeng went through the same thing at age two. After the divorce papers were signed, Dengdeng went to live with Cheng Shuyao, and Yao Yao stayed with her mother. The family was thus split in two and Shangguan Yunzhu began to co-habit with He Lu. Subsequently, the Shanghai Film Studio banned Shangguan Yunzhu from acting for five years as a punishment for her illicit relationship with He Lu.

Again, Yao Yao lost someone she could call Dad. This time, she was nine years old.

She stayed behind with her mother, with whom she dared not act the pampered little girl. They lived in an exquisite and elegant Spanish-style apartment building, on the top of which were two small Gothic windows with white lacy curtains drawn behind them most of the time. In the faint rays of the sun in an overcast sky, the curtains emitted an air of serene refinement reminiscent of a Jane Austen novel. The building was divided into four units. Yao Yao's family occupied a unit on the third floor. It was the largest unit in the building, with a spacious uncovered terrace overlooking the garden. To all appearances, Yao Yao lived the same life as before, still taking piano lessons from a teacher in Xujiahui, still an undistinguished student of piano and still getting mediocre grades at her elementary school.

There was a glass-paneled wrought-iron door at the top of the stairs. On sunny days, the intricate patterns on the door cast their shadows on the flight of stairs. Her nurse, who had always slept with her, was gone. Her brother and his nurse with her rich supply of stories were also gone. She climbed the stairs alone.

The stairwell was usually very quiet. On the second floor lived Dong Zhujun, owner of the Jinjiang Restaurant, who had moved there only recently from a house with a large garden. She was, at that time, often staying at home on sick leave. Daughter of a maidservant and a coolie who pulled flatbed carts, she had been sold by her parents into a brothel but, through her own hard work, she came to own the only Sichuan-style restaurant in Shanghai at the time, a restaurant so popular that even grandees like the famous gang boss Du Yuesheng had to wait for a table. Her restaurant later expanded into a hotel, with a pedestrians' overpass linking the old building with the new. It was the only overpass of its kind in the French Concession. Like Shangguan Yunzhu, she was also a legendary figure in Shanghai. During the five years in which Shangguan Yunzhu was banned from the movie screen, her neighbor downstairs, the "red" capitalist Dong Zhujun, donated the Jinjiang to the Shanghai Municipal Government, to be used for accommodations for dignitaries. She herself eventually was reduced to an advisory role, with no real power.

Yao Yao would quietly pass by her door.

Sometimes Yao Yao would run into that beautiful and graceful woman on the stairs. Every time this happened, Yao Yao would step aside and drop her eyes. She seldom struck up conversations with people for fear of being asked about what was happening at home, and she shunned topics that might bring her painful memories. She had no idea that her closely guarded secrets were, in fact, all too trivial to the woman on the second floor. Even if she had heard the raucous sounds from upstairs and known that Yao Yao's mother had boxed her father's ears, she would have taken these things to be nothing more than a wavelet in a stormy sea. Yao Yao did not cry when these things happened. She just watched silently from an unobtrusive corner until the nurse led her away. Even though Mother's doings were not much of a secret to the general public, she never discussed them with anyone.

On rainy days, the red bricks of the outdoor stairs looked heartwarming under the raindrops. Since everyone she knew well had moved away, Yao Yao asked that she be allowed to play with her brother Dengdeng after he got home from his boarding kindergarten, so that she could stay for some hours at Cheng Shuyao's home. Once given permission, she would open the glass-paneled wrought-iron door and fly down the red-brick stairs. On her way, she would pass by a brownish red building where the eccentric scholar of Chinese studies, Xiong Shili, lived. He was often lamenting over the scarcity of successors to his career. Further down was a house embowered in green foliage, the residence of the Guo family who owned Wing On (Yong An) Department Store. When the department store became a joint state-private enterprise, the Guos invited a Beijing opera troupe home for a performance of *The Highway Men of Shandong*. Past the house was a small triangle park, whose pink and white blossomed oleander bushes emitted a strange, heady odor. Children claim that oleander blossoms are poisonous and that because their odor could kill people, one should hold one's breath when passing under them. Yao Yao must have done the same thing. She would then enter a wide alley, where Cheng Shuyao had rented a large room on the second floor of an ordinary-looking house.

As all children of broken families are prone to do, she steered clear of the subject of the divorce. Once at Cheng Shuyao's home, she still called him Dad in her endearing way and still played with her brother as if nothing had happened. After night fell, she would return home, happily.

When asked about Yao Yao, her high-school classmate Yuebo said, "Are you asking about Cheng Yaoyao? Well, she was a quiet girl. I never had much to do with her. I was a hyperactive kid and kept my distance from quiet girls like her. As far as I remember, she wasn't someone to kid around with. She'd burst into tears."

Soon thereafter, Cheng Shuyao sent Dengdeng to his own parents in Beijing because he was going to marry Wu Yan, a well-known figure in Shanghai's high society. Yao Yao could go to Cheng Shuyao's home only when Dengdeng was in Shanghai on summer vacation. In fact, Shangguan Yunzhu had never stopped Yao Yao from visiting Dengdeng, but Yao Yao never let on to her mother her wishes to see anyone other than her brother at the Cheng household. Some time later, Dong Zhujun, the woman downstairs, consulted Shangguan about a relocation deal, whereupon the latter moved to another apartment building in the same neighborhood.

By the time they left that exquisite little building, the ban on Shangguan Yunzhu had already been lifted. Her successful performance as a guerilla fighter in the movie *The Winds of the South Sea* won recognition from all the officials and her colleagues in the movie industry. Her success greatly heartened the movie stars of old Shanghai, instilling in them hopes for their own chances at adapting to the new generation of movies. So she gained a firm foothold as an actor valued by the Communist Party. In January 1956, she was escorted, on short notice, to the Sino-Soviet Friendship Building. A Stalinist-style building erected on the ruins of Hardoon Park, it had a slender and pointed steeple that sent a red star that glittered into the clouds at night. In the high-ceilinged main hall, she saw Chairman Mao Zedong. She is said to have written on her calendar, "Tonight, I had the happiness of seeing our dear Chairman Mao. I will forever cherish the memory."

After graduating from elementary school, Yao Yao tested into the Music School affiliated with the Shanghai Conservatory of Music, to study piano.

"She was petite and delicate, like her mother. One look at her told you that she lived a sheltered life. Her clothes were very nice. Everything she used was the most expensive of its kind, and she always wore leather shoes, something few girls did in those days. Most wore home-made cloth shoes. She was very fair. Her fingers were nice and white. She always tried to hide her style of living at her home, but sometimes she gave herself away in unguarded moments," said Zhong Wan, raising one eyebrow. A schoolmate of Yao Yao's, she was a vocalist and kept a big, ringing voice. "In those days, improvement of personal integrity was the order of the day. Hard work and plain-living were sources of pride, while a high style of living was against the tide of the times. But those schoolmates with distinguished family backgrounds remained a little different from run-of-the-mill schoolmates. Her mother being a famous movie actress, Yao Yao led a more affluent life than average. Although smug about it, she also knew that it was not the right attitude, so she often tried to cover it up."

After many attempts, I finally found some of Yao Yao's writings, among which was a thin red-lined pad whose pages had turned brownish. It was a self-appraisal that she wrote upon graduation. With a pointed fountain pen, she summed up her years at the Music School on the kind of inferior coarse paper manufactured in the 1960s, which contained yellowish blotches of un-pulverized straw. If you were to pull out the remnants of the straw, you would leave tiny holes in the paper. Her penmanship was neat and unaffected, her attitude sincere and modest. In that summary, she wrote that she was a weak-willed person. "I do better if I make friends with highly motivated classmates, but if I keep the company of classmates with low motivation, I fall behind.... During the first three years of junior high, I was content with staying in the middle and unwilling to change the status quo. When I was promoted to senior high, I heard complaints that my grades were not good enough for the promotion. I was frightened and shocked, but as time wore on, I forgot about it. Soon after the new semester started, I began to cling to classmates with the wrong kind of ideas and couldn't concentrate on my studies. My grades slipped. I did not share my thoughts with the teachers. I did not care about the communal interest. I kept silent at political study sessions. I could not answer questions in class. I could not complete the piano class assignments. I didn't open my heart to classmates. In short, I became a bad student. I went astray. At this critical juncture, the teachers and the school authorities repeatedly talked with me to help me turn around. My classmates held a panel discussion expressly to help me analyze my situation. I did some self-criticism and said I was more than willing to accept their criticism and rectify my mistakes."

Dengdeng told me, "I remember how my mother hit my sister one summer. That day, Mom had been scolding Sister during a meal. Sister was standing behind Mom, fanning her. At the height of her anger, Mom turned around and gave Sister a slap across the face. Mom didn't talk loud, but once her face darkened, she looked very formidable. Mom continued with her meal while Sister went on fanning her, saying nothing and looking at no one. I was scared. I hid behind a tall-backed sofa in the living room and peeked out. Sister did not cry. There was no expression on her face. She looked perfectly unruffled."

"Why did your mother scold her and hit her?" I asked.

"On the surface, it was because Sister lost the new watch that Mom had just bought her, but in fact it was because Sister had a crush on a boy in her class."

Ye Yuren, Yao Yao's classmate, said in reminiscence, "I heard that Yao Yao had written a letter to that boy, saying that she liked Tolstoy's novel *Resurrection* and asked him out, to see the Russian-made movie based on the novel." In those days, Sino-Soviet relations being as cordial as they were, Chinese students loved watching Russian movies, like *White Nights, The Idiot, Resurrection, The Red Sail,* and *Anna on the Neck. The Red sail* was a sentimental romance story, about the red sail boat of a prince sailing on the blue sea to bring home a girl that he had met only by chance.

It was a letter that any girl in love could have written. Mildly worded but, to some extent, passionate and tactless, it was a letter that could have come from most girls of that age, but most girls would not have taken the initiative and would have written only in response. Such letters share similar themes and feelings. Any reader can sense from the ill-chosen words the eager palpitations of a heart awakening from all its innocence.

It surprises me that, for someone who had grown up as a witness to so much bitter fighting between lovers, Yao Yao was still able to express herself so eagerly and bravely, and to expect solace from love affairs. She had much more resilience than I would have given her credit for. Maybe someone like her craved someone who could love her and be passionately loved by her. At puberty, the longing for love may indeed be stronger than everything else and, like boiling milk that can rise and spill over the pot in one minute, it results in a mess which can be hard to clean up.

This did eventually happen to Yao Yao one day.

"Yes, I remember," said Zhong Wan. "That young man was always in a pale blue jacket. He was not that good-looking. I remember him as thin, small, with a fair-complexion, but quite fashion-conscious, and he rode a very nice bicycle to school. He was an excellent student of piano but politically unmotivated and didn't seem to care very much about anything. He never tried to join the Communist Youth League, and he didn't seem to hobnob with classmates."

Such was the very first young man Yao Yao had fallen for.

Yao Yao's grades were unimpressive but her family background, in political terms, was better than that of the young man. Mao Zedong's meetings with Shangguan Yunzhu freed her from the yet undisclosed list of people to be labeled Rightists in the Shanghai Film Studio in 1957. It is said that after Shangguan Yunzhu was dropped from that list, another colleague was put on the list to fill the quota and, soon after the official announcement, was sent to a labor-reform farm in Qinghai, as was Yuebo's sister. Shortly thereafter, Shangguan Yunzhu went abroad with a delegation of Chinese film industry professionals to participate in an international film festival. Whenever foreign counterparts came to China to visit, she was invariably put on the reception team. In the 1960s when China was closed to the outside world and the average Chinese citizen was not supposed to have any contact with foreigners, Shangguan was given the highest trust and honor. Those were good years for her.

An unsophisticated girl could easily develop a crush on a flawed but remarkable member of the opposite sex, in much the same way a beauty would fall for a beast. I wonder if Yao Yao harbored the same kind of soft sentiments. In Yao Yao's case, these sentiments were mixed with compassion and sympathy as well as admiration for a good pianist. I also wonder if Yao Yao was enamored of his sophistication or was intoxicated with her own tender feelings. Any human mind can be dark and twisted, let alone that of Yao Yao who had grown up in such complex surroundings.

The object of her admiration surrendered her letter to the class president. Ye Yuren, who had been Yao Yao's fellow piano student, commented that the young man was probably afraid that her passion would suffocate him. But Zhong Wan believed that the young man was afraid of violating school regulations, according to which students who dated were punishable by expulsion. His family background being what it was, he had to exercise caution. As for Yuebo, he believed that the young man did not like Yao Yao at all. If he did, he would have had the necessary courage.

Rumors about Yao Yao's letter spread throughout the school overnight. In contrast to the frank and straightforward Zhong Wan whose father was a movie actor once active in the pre-1949 Liberated Areas, Yao Yao had the vanity and the feminine wiles of a girl brought up by old-Shanghai entertainers. Sometimes she tried to cover up her family circumstances and sometimes to show off, wishing to exhibit her difference from others while, at the same time, to be taken as a naive and simple girl, as most of her female schoolmates were. Driven by these conflicting emotions, she turned herself into a two-faced outsider in the eyes of schoolmates with the simple peasant values of the 1960s, and proved to be no less a two-faced outsider to the children of the overthrown class quietly resisting their fate with youthful waywardness. Everyone looked at her askance, in apprehension and in alarm, with a vague feeling that she had something to hide. No one had any real sympathy for her. Perhaps that was why her classmates held a meeting to criticize and analyze her.

Zhong Wan said, "Yao Yao had very fair, translucent skin. Upon the slightest provocation, she would redden all the way to her eyelids, and her skin looked as if it was about to tear open. She was the very image of a frail and delicate young lady. However ..." Here, Zhong Wan had an awkward pause before deciding to continue, "However, there was talk among schoolmates at the time that Yao Yao was a little ... easy, and was often quite uninhibited in male company. When the mood seized her, she would hug a male classmate from behind. That's the way she was. That was something nobody did in those days. People commented that it was because she had inherited her mother's easy virtue."

Zhong Wan had slurred over the word "easy," as if her clear and ringing voice had caught when she was taking a breath, as if she hated to say it out loud. To those who had spent their youth in the 1960s with its campaign to learn from Lei Feng, this was a major accusation and a show of contempt, and it was a word capable of multiple meanings. Zhong Wan looked at me in embarrassment, apologetic and awkward for having dredged up unpleasant memories, but she was delivering on her promise that she would tell me everything she knew. In the beginning, I had no idea what that promise meant to Zhong Wan. It was when Yao Yao's long-eyebrowed smiling face began to turn as pale as a wintry moon later in our conversation that I came to realize that Yao Yao was not a pleasant or relaxing topic to bring up.

In Ye Yuren's words, "Yao Yao was absent from

school for two days out of shame and anger, and spent her time crying under her quilt at home. It was only after our teacher said things like friendship between schoolmates were more precious than gold that she calmed down." By that time, Ye Yuren had already switched from his piano major to bassoon in preparation for skipping a grade, so that he could major in conducting, as the Music School asked of him. That was in 1963. He was a high achiever and was fortunate enough to be born of a parent who had been a writer as an underground member of the Communist Party before Liberation.

But did Yao Yao really calm down? This is what she wrote on that pad of paper: "In spite of all appearances, I was in fact in a great deal of agony. I believed I was the most worthless student in my class and in the whole school. Everybody looked down on me. These thoughts intensified whenever I read the comments on my character in the school reports. I had nothing good about me, neither grades nor personal integrity. I had nothing but warts all over me. My inferiority complex was like a burden that kept my head weighted down. I was determined to behave myself in the future and not to let out a peep about anything. It was just impossible for me to get far."

Was this why Shangguan Yunzhu slapped her across the face? Dengdeng from his perch behind the tall-backed sofa saw how angry his mother was. Was she angry because Yao Yao was accused of being flirtatious or because Yao Yao was in love, or because Yao Yao had acted inappropriately? Or, was it because the only beloved child living with her was so careless with her own reputation and so oblivious of the fact that life was now a precarious journey for them?

"Later, when our school authorities began to put greater emphasis on ideology, I started to watch out for my political awareness, and yet, because I had no idea how to balance ideology and professional competence, my grades suffered. Regardless, I set a higher bar on myself but, out of a sense of inferiority, I dared not make public pronouncements or take actions that might draw attention. My piano professor cared a lot for me. She helped me draw up a personal plan, a plan that I was determined to carry out in secret. If I were to blab it out, people would accuse me of being boastful and even say in ridicule, 'Poor thing!

You call this an attempt at self-improvement?' So I kept quiet. This goes to show what a petty-bourgeois mentality I had, giving up on myself like that. At the same time, I harbored thoughts of surprising people by showing them what a change I had made to myself. But I didn't make much headway. Without help from the group, I failed in my go-it-alone approach.

"My new piano professor found major problems with the way I played the instrument. My hands ached because my method was incorrect. So the professor took me to the teaching and research group of the Conservatory to get their diagnosis. They decided to demote me one grade and put me on dry and dull basic training again. I was caught by surprise. I just couldn't start over like that. Were they serious? So I wanted to give up piano. I had so many problems in my playing, my fingers were too weak, my hands too small, my ears not attuned to music. Piano was just too hard for me. I developed an interest in drama and wanted to switch majors, but my mother and the teachers said no, especially my piano professor, who insisted that I needed only to be motivated and try harder. Thanks to their admonition, my own wish to make something of myself, and some soul-searching on my part, I dismissed my improper thoughts and settled down to pursue my study of piano."

Zhang Xiaoxiao said, "Yao Yao did tell me that she didn't like piano and wanted to stop playing, but her mother and the teachers at the school wouldn't hear of it, so she had to go on. I had thought that she was a good student at school and a cut above the rest. So when I heard her say such things, I thought she must have been unhappy about something else and was thus not to be taken seriously."

Zhong Wan, her classmate, said, "Yao Yao's grades were mediocre, to say the least."

So the études that Dengdeng heard Yao Yao play every day at home in Shanghai were, in fact, her school assignments meant to rebuild her basic skills. In Yao Yao's own words, "I attributed my aversion to piano to my fear of hardships but, in fact, it brought to light my bourgeois way of thinking. I had to be able to look at my problems from an elevated political perspective before it was possible to reform myself." The youth in those days were supposed to look on what they didn't like or weren't good at doing as political problems and engage in self-criticism. Having grown up in such an environment, was Yao Yao still the fragile girl who easily got teary upon the slightest provocation, as Yuebo remembered her?

"She looked happy. When girls got together and shrieked in delight, she always joined the excitement. But if you looked closely, you would have seen that she was, deep down, not as happy as she tried to look," said Zhong Wan. "I was once involved in a school play with her. She played the role of an underground Communist messenger pursued by the enemy. With so much time spent together, I got to see that sometimes when she was trying very hard to tell a joke, her laughter was fake." Zhong Wan was by no means the only one with such feelings because, in evaluations on Yao Yao's character, there were comments about her "not having enough trust in her comrades," and she was asked to "overcome that shortcoming" in the following semester.

So Yao Yao was trying to make herself out to be a girl without a worry, whose life was a picture of perfection. Since she was at an age when one starts dreaming about the future, the kind of image she tried to project perhaps represented what she wanted for her future life. In order to play the part well, she tried her best to hide the reality of her life, just as Zhong Wan said. She did not seem to be aware that if you try to act like someone you are not, you could be perceived by people around you as lacking in sincerity. Among the young, the insincere gained no friends, as the frank and straightforward Zhong Wan had said when I first sat down with her at her home. I started by saying, "I heard that you were good friends?"

She replied, sitting upright, "I may be counted as one who knew Yao Yao well, but in fact even I got to know only one part of her. I can't say that I understood her. We didn't really open our hearts to each other."

The pains Yao Yao had taken to be something she was not had cost her a potential friend.

Where did she get the urge to appear perfect? She had already begun to rebel against her mother, so it could not have been imposed on her by her mother. The idea was all her own. I recall a poem written by a young girl saying that the rivers were in their riverbeds, the little birds were in their nests, the clouds were in the blue sky, the flowers were on their stems, the babies were in their cradles, God was in Heaven, and everything in the world was in its proper place. Such was her world. Yao Yao, a girl who had experienced turbulence in her childhood, wanted to bring everybody happiness in a perfect life.

After graduating from the Music School, Yao Yao failed the entrance exam for the Shanghai Conservatory of Music. The school authorities wanted her to go to an army-run farm in Xinjiang to dedicate her youth to the construction of that frontier region. Yao Yao refused. A few months later, Shangguan Yunzhu took her to the Ear, Eye, Nose and Throat Hospital for an examination of her vocal chords. Subsequently, Professor Zhou Xiaoyan of the Shanghai Conservatory of Music took her on as a student in the Vocal Arts Department to be trained as a lyric soprano. It was 1964. Yao Yao left home and moved into the girls' dormitory of the Conservatory in a big Western-style house near Middle Huaihai Road. Nobody knew who had owned this house, nor its exact architectural style featuring several onion-shaped spires. Yao Yao took up residence in one of the rooms tucked beneath the spires.

Away from home and free from the piano, Yao Yao suddenly blossomed into a cheerful and lively girl, joining in the fun and laughter at the Conservatory. She became a member of the drama team and took on the roles of revolutionaries. Zhong Wan said, "When acting out the roles of revolutionaries, she went out of her way to be forceful in her movements and passionate in her facial expressions, trying her level best to reproduce the inspiring image of a revolutionary. But she just didn't have the look."

She was keen on improving her political standing and tried to join the Communist Youth League. During the Learn-from-Lei Feng Campaign, she declared at a mass meeting of the Conservatory that she had as many as thirteen woolen sweaters but was ready to learn from Lei Feng and change to a frugal way of life. This declaration shocked her fellow students. In those days, anyone who owned a couple of woolen sweaters was considered well-off. Imagine that she had thirteen! But everybody was impressed by her sincerity in going so far as to make such a public disclosure. On her own initiative, she offered comments on her mother's egoistic ideas about career and her mother's hunger for fame and gain. Then she went on to tell the audience that, in her view, the many things her mother bought for her were meant to corrupt her. As a result, Yao Yao was elected an Exemplary Learner of Lei Feng in her freshman year and later she became a member of the Communist Youth League. In her exhilaration, she made a habit of proudly displaying her Youth League badge on her outer garment at all times.

Soon after the Cultural Revolution began in 1966, Yao Yao was among the first to be labeled an "offspring of the five black evil elements." Students of the Conservatory formed one group of Red Guards after another. At one time, there were more than a hundred "battle teams." The passion cultivated by music flared like raging flames. The atmosphere gradually turned heated and cruel. There were in the Conservatory quite a number of "offspring of the five evil elements" like Yao Yao, who, before long, came to be called by the revolutionaries "educable offspring." Those who had severed all ties with their parents remained eligible for membership as Red Guards. Many indicated readiness to do so. Yao Yao put up a large-character poster at the Shanghai Film Studio denouncing her mother, and stopped going home. At that time, Shangguan had just undergone a major brain surgery and walked with a limp, but she was forced to leave the hospital and participate in the revolutionary campaign at the Film Studio.

Soon thereafter, some Conservatory students, mostly offspring of high-level officials, joined the Kang Da Battle Team (Kang Da is short for Chinese People's Anti-Japanese Military and Political University, set up initially in Yan'an in 1937). It was a Red Guard organization put together by the Shanghai Municipal Red Guards Revolutionary Committee and was one of the first rebel organizations in the universities and colleges of Shanghai. By contrast, the organization open to "educable offspring" was a peripheral organization called "Red Comrades-in-Arms." Yao Yao and Zhong Wan spent three days and nights in a classroom writing big-character posters, the way regular Red Guards did, to expose the pernicious influence of the old educational system on young people. In the meantime, they decided to join "Red Comrades-in-Arms."

"Didn't you ever feel sleepy?" I asked.

"No, not at all. On the contrary, we had a wonderful time," said Zhong Wan affably. "In spite of her delicate looks, Yao Yao proved to be quite tough."

It was then that Yao Yao got to know Yan Kai, a tall and dashing young man, son of revolutionary cadres, student in the Department of Traditional Chinese Instruments, and a leader of the Kang Da Team.

Nobody can recall where Yao Yao got a Red Guard outfit for herself: a grass-green army uniform, an old-fashioned hard-rimmed army cap, an aluminum Chairman Mao badge, and a canvass army belt with a brass buckle. Many Red Guards had struck people with such belts and Red Guards at the film studio had struck Shangguan Yunzu with them. A slap across her face had sent the movie star staggering back quite a few paces before collapsing to the floor, at a time when she had been so gravely ill that she could not even think straight.

That autumn, in the midst of the raging flames of revolution, Yao Yao and Zhong Wan, sporting the afore-described outfits, went to Beijing by train, free of charge, for Chairman Mao's fourth review of Red

Guards. After the Cultural Revolution began, Mao
Zedong, wearing a Red Guard armband, had led
other leaders of the country in reviewing feverishly
excited Red Guards at Tiananmen Square. After the
first of such reviews in the summer, students from
all over the country began to descend on Beijing.
The government issued emergency notifications to
railways stations throughout the country, instructing
them to let students ride free of charge to Beijing to
see Chairman Mao, and local governments were to
provide all necessary facilities for the students. As
children under ten were not allowed to go, a children's
song suddenly spread throughout the streets and
alleys: "We want to join the Revolutionary National
Network Campaign. Why doesn't the Shanghai
Government let us go?"

The train platforms were dark with masses
of Beijing-bound students, all dressed in similar
outfits. Some kept feeling for the Chairman Mao
badges pinned to their chests, lest they lose them in
the jostling crowd. Once the doors became blocked
by passengers trying to get aboard, people began to
climb into the trains through the windows, the most

agile ones being students of the Sports Institute. The railway cars were filled to bursting with people sitting and standing. Even the luggage racks were used as seats. After even the space under the seats was taken up by people lying down, new arrivals began to sit on the thin seat-backs. But these were not refugees; they were all young people reciting and singing quotations from Chairman Mao. They were all Red Guards loving one another across gender lines. The trains, as packed as they were, made all the local stops, to pick up more Red Guards eager to see Chairman Mao. There was no food, no drinks, no working toilets, not even water with which to wash their faces. The trains reeked with body odor, the offensive smell of sweat, and the foul stink of human excrement. Upon arriving in Beijing after three days and nights like this, they learned that all the trains to Beijing were in the same sorry condition.

Thanks to the Red Guard reception station, Zhong Wan and Yao Yao found their way to a huge classroom in the Central Conservatory of Music already filled with students lying on the floor, awaiting Chairman Mao's review on Tiananmen Square. The two of them were led to a small vacant spot.

Zhong Wan plopped down. This was the first time in three days that she managed to lie down.

Yao Yao also lay down, only to sit up again immediately, because next to her slept a girl from a small town in the North, whose hair, all entangled, was giving off a stench. "She must have fleas!" said Yao Yao, rocking Zhong Wan.

"I'm dead tired," said Zhong Wan. "Can't you just tough it out?"

"I can't," said Yao Yao, continuing to rock Zhong Wan, intending to move to another spot.

But where could they move to? The room was filled to spilling over. And Yao Yao was showing contempt for a Red Guard. Zhong Wan was enraged.

Yao Yao dropped her eyes and stopped insisting.

The dead tired young men and women who filled up the unfamiliar classroom slept like logs that night. Everyone's dreams were haunted with the grinding of teeth of those who had roundworms in their bellies, the snores of those fast asleep, the coughs of those who had caught a cold on the road, the stench of Huili sneakers soaked with sweat, and the dry smell of the crisp night air of Beijing. Upon waking up in the morning, Zhong Wan found Yao Yao sitting, as before. She just could not bring herself to lie down and sleep.

Yao Yao saw Chairman Mao on Tiananmen Square. When the open-top limousine with Chairman Mao standing in it slowly drew near, the hundreds of thousands of people on the Square burst into thunderous cheers. Everybody shouted "Long live Chairman Mao!" and shed tears of excitement.

"Did Yao Yao also cry?" I asked.

"Oh yes! She cried her eyes out! In those days, who wouldn't shed happy tears at the sight of Chairman Mao? She shouted until she was hoarse without even remembering what she had shouted. Now, a trained vocalist shouting herself hoarse; just imagine how fervently she shouted. It was indeed a case of being ready to 'drop dead' from happiness."

Taking time off from her activities in Beijing, Yao Yao had gone to see Dengdeng in his high school. Emerging from a hallway pasted over with big-character posters and Chairman Mao's portraits, Dengdeng had become a quiet 15-year-old and a voracious reader of his grandfather's collection of books. Having been brought up with all due decorum in his grandfather's home, he felt a little envious of his sister whom his mother had slapped for having a crush on a boy.

Standing at the entrance of the school, they had talked amid the powerful music blasting from the loudspeakers.

They mentioned their mother.

Yao Yao told her brother that Mother was beaten at a harsh denouncement session because of her movie-star status and also because Chairman Mao had seen her alone.

"But wasn't that an honor?" asked Dengdeng in astonishment.

Yao Yao kept silent.

Thirty-four years later, I asked Dengdeng, when he was a 49-year-old editor, "Did she tell you that she had put up a big-character poster at the film studio announcing her severance of all ties with your mother?"

"No."

"When she told you about your mother being denounced, did she look worried or sad?"

"No, she did not."

"Did she tell you what she was doing in Beijing?"

"She said she was joining the big National Network Campaign."

"She didn't say she was there for Chairman Mao's fourth review of Red Guards?"

"No."

"How did she look?"

"She looked happy. And she seemed to be busy. She left after only a short talk."

Yao Yao did not tell Zhong Wan about this visit with her brother.

At that time, the Red Guards' Revolutionary Committee of Shanghai put together a file on Zhang Chunqiao (a member of the Gang of Four), describing his "counter-revolutionary past." The Kang Da Team of the Conservatory put together a file on "counter-revolutionary" Yu Huiyong, the one-time chair of the Department of Traditional Chinese Instruments. Both had been powerful men during the Cultural Revolution. The Red Guards' Revolutionary Committee of Shanghai also addressed a letter to Chairman Mao's wife Jiang

Qing, accusing her of having appointed the "wrong people" and let class enemies worm their way into revolutionary ranks. Subsequently, Zhang Chunqiao dispatched People's Liberation Army's Mao Zedong Thought Propaganda Teams and Factory Workers' Mao Zedong Thought Propaganda Teams to take over all universities and colleges that had branches of the Shanghai Red Guards Revolutionary Committee, to punish the students and disband the Committee. The key figures of the Committee were locked up as counter-revolutionaries.

The Kang Da Battle Team that Yao Yao belonged to decided to organize "propaganda squads" to go to East Sea islands and coastal spots in the Northern Jiangsu region, to spread Mao Zedong Thought and perform revolutionary songs and dances for troops that were stationed at outposts there. Yao Yao went home, took some clothes, and left with the "squad." By this time, big-character posters vilifying Shang-guan Yunzhu covered the walls from the stairwell at the street entrance all the way up to the door of Apartment 29. The posters were full of filthy abuse offensive to any decent eye. The entire hallway reeked with the unpleasant smell of paper, glue, and ink, a smell that Yao Yao found familiar. The apartment had been raided numerous times. Anybody could just walk in. There was a time when the front door was not even supposed to stay closed. Groups of students were followed by factory workers and Neighborhood Committee members. Even if idlers from the streets came in for a raid, nobody would have dared block them. They wanted gold-nibbed pens and money, and walked away with everything that struck their fancy. Before leaving, they hit and yelled at the shaking and trembling Shangguan Yunzhu. The squeaky clean and orderly home was now a mess. Shangguan Yunzhu had been beaten black and blue all over. There were also internal injuries caused by iron bars wrapped up with rubber, injuries that left no traces on the skin. Those who had beaten her forbade her to disclose what they had been trying to get out of her and forbade her to tell anyone that she had been beaten during interrogation. "I can't tell those things, not even if I die," said Shangguan to Yao Yao.

Soon thereafter, Yao Yao left Shanghai with her squad. Those classmates who knew about Shangguan's health problems advised her to stay and take care of her mother, but she replied, "She doesn't want me to stay."

Yao Yao left with her classmates. That performance tour had a particularly tight schedule with very little personal time. Only when they were on their way to the next stop on a long-distance bus were they able to indulge in some good-humored banter. However, Yao Yao, who had been lively and cheerful, did not join the chatter and the laughter. She was "surprisingly quiet," according to Ye Yuren, who had just found his first love in Zhong Wan. He was on the same tour but had never had much to do with Yao Yao. Looking at her, he felt that "she had suddenly withdrawn into a silent unknown world all her own."

Yao Yao was now in love with Yan Kai. He was a proud young man, proud of his revolutionary father, of the vision of his father's contemporaries, of their tenacity, of the revolutionary blood in his own veins, proud for his future career as a successor to the revolutionary cause, and for being the staunchest revolutionary. Children of cadres of that era, especially boys, had the greatest pride in their fathers and their fathers' cause. Such father-son ties were never to be seen again. In a young man, such pride was very attractive.

Their love, lasting from winter to spring, was of a kind that intoxicated even the onlookers. "It was like what we saw in foreign films. I was also in love at that time, but I was never anywhere near what they were like," recounted Zhong Wan with a slightly shy and hesitant smile, as if she was pleasantly surprised and a little scared. It was like the smile of an embarrassed Chinese kid at the sight of embracing lovers. "They were deeply, deeply in love, something rarely seen in those days."

In the spring of 1968, all Chinese, male and female, adults and children, wore the same kind of blue cotton outfits. Those whose love affairs were exposed by anonymous big-character posters were, male and female alike, denounced and pilloried. Those who couldn't stand the humiliation aged overnight and killed themselves before dawn arrived. When large swathes of canola flowers turned yellow in the moist fields in Qingpu and nerves were most vulnerable, some people just snapped. It was a spring where fragile humaneness was swept away in the name of revolution.

Children who had experienced such a season were likely to later become cold and indifferent.

The tall and handsome Yan Kai would lift Yao Yao and spin her around in front of their schoolmates. Yao Yao would give way to peals of laughter and blush furiously. In late spring, Yao Yao moved into Yan Kai's practice room. Gossip about them soon spread throughout the Conservatory, saying that they were together day and night, and that Yao Yao often stayed away from her dorm night after night. This was such an un-heard-of thing that people around them were at a loss as to how to react. Some pretended not to have heard anything. Ye Yuren, being close to them, would tease them about it, and their faces would glow with delight. Ye Yuren said to me, "That was happiness. Yao Yao was a woman who had enjoyed happiness."

"She must have been pleased. She must have thrown all caution to the winds, and therefore had nothing to fear," I said.

Zhong Wan replied, "Yes, of course. And she wasn't just pleased. They were really happy. In our 'squad,' there were a few other pairs of lovers, but none had their kind of passion."

"Why were they like that?" I asked.

"They just couldn't keep a check on themselves. Students of music just find it hard to hide their emotions," said Zhong Wan.

They gave free rein to their passion. In that spring when abstinence and self-denial were the order of the day, their defiance was like a flower in winter that blossomed out of season and tried to be as luxuriant as a spring bloom. Yan Kai's father had also come under attack and was labeled a capitalist roader. He was stripped of his power and denounced, and his home was raided. By this time, the rebels had acquired experience, and so had the victims. In the compound where Yan Kai lived, the families of the victims burned letters and photographs in advance of the raids, and the young males organized themselves into "Home Defense Teams" and came to blows with the hot-eyed rebels. The rebels called them "tiny mantises trying to stop a mighty chariot." In fact, that observation was right on the mark.

Yao Yao and Yan Kai, who rarely went home, spent their days and nights in Yan Kai's small practice room, oblivious to the outside world.

Early in the morning of November 23, 1968, Zhong Wan heard someone cry in the hallway, "Wei Yao! (Yao Yao's official name at school) Something happened at your home. Go back, quick!"

Prior to this, a student called Tang Qun was also told to go home one early morning, only to find that her mother had committed suicide.

Zhong Wan rose from bed, opened her door, and saw Yao Yao rushing down from upstairs. Many female students had risen and were standing by their doors, watching her. Yao Yao kept her eyes down, her face expressionless. Without looking at anyone, she followed the messenger from the Conservatory down the stairs.

Someone who had grown up in the neighborhood asked me, "Are you going to write about Shangguan Yunzhu's suicide?" Ten years old in 1968, he later graduated from the History Department of Fudan University. "If you are going to write about her suicide, please include the details that I've heard about. She jumped and happened to land in the basket of a vegetable farmer sitting on the sidewalk. It was before daybreak, and the food market was not yet open. So the farmer was waiting under her window. You remember the kind of large baskets in food markets back when we were little? Each of those baskets, woven with iron wire, was as large as a round table. It so happened that she landed smack into that farmer's basket which was full of fresh green bok choy, the kind that easily cooks tender, and was just in season in November. Her blood dyed the bok choy red. She was still able to speak at first and told the farmer where she lived. You know what happened to that basketful of bok choy? The market venders hosed off the blood and sold the bok choy to unsuspecting customers."

We were eating in a restaurant when he said this. A 14-year-old girl at our table screamed and said, "Oh stop it! We are eating!"

Yan Kai went with Yao Yao from the Conservatory to her home. Her stepfather said that Shangguan had already been sent to the hospital. By the time they got to the hospital, they were told that she had already died and that the corpse had been sent to the crematorium. Once there, they were told that the body had already been cremated along with the bodies of other dead counter-revolutionaries, and no ashes were given to them.

Three months later, Yao Yao and other students of the graduating class were sent to an army farm in Liyang, the poorest area in Jiangsu Province. It was said that the dogs there fed on human excrement. There being no lavatories, whenever a dog saw a human crouch down, it would wait off to one side, its hungry eyes wide open. Often, before the human had quite stood up, the dog would pounce. The Conservatory students, with the nutritious food, however limited, that they had brought from Shanghai, became the dogs' favorites. And then there were the swarms of mosquitoes. As Yao Yao's blood sugar level was higher than average, the mosquitoes flocked to her. When it was her turn on night watch duty, she seemed to be completely covered in a cape made of mosquitoes. And yet, each of the photographs taken of her on the farm—I wonder by whom—showed her smiling. With a hand in an upper garment pocket, her head tilted slightly to one side, she looked like an optimistic revolutionary with a toughness that was absent from the photographs taken by the side of West Lake on a leisurely summer day when she was in love. All the hardships she was experiencing were concealed in that one smile. As for the photos by West Lake, they were the work of Yan Kai. At that time, her mother was being beaten cruelly by investigators from Beijing. Yao Yao rarely went home. She sat on the iron chains by the willowy lakeside against a background of a white stone bridge over long ripples glittering in the sun. It was a typical scene of the gentle local landscape. She was wearing the same smile. But a closer look revealed that the softness in her face in the West Lake photos was due to less effort in that smile. Also, there was a trace of fear and helplessness in the softness. Her mother was still living in agony at that time. But now, she was an orphan, away from her native town and her lover, and a poverty-stricken orphan, too. When her classmates couldn't take that kind of life anymore and fled back to Shanghai one after another, she stayed behind to hold on to her wages. Was it for all these reasons that she did her best to keep up the smile in every photograph?

On March 8, 1970, the Workers' Propaganda Team at the Conservatory took Yao Yao into custody for investigation. Day after day, they interrogated her on her relationship with Yan Kai and what they had done together. She said, "We did what you do with your wives."

She was released after two months. Only then did she see the package of food that Yan Kai had sent her two months before. There were a large bag of Ovaltine, cans of luncheon meat and anchovies, and a small bottle of mosquito repellent oil. Upon returning to Shanghai, Yao Yao learned that Yan Kai had slashed his own arteries and died one day before she was taken into custody. The Conservatory had launched the brutal campaign of "purging the class ranks." All members of the faculty and student body were sent to an enclosed setting in the countryside with no permission to return home. All requests to leave the village needed be approved by authorities at the Conservatory level. Yan Kai was denounced as member of a small counter-revolutionary clique. He found a very sharp old-fashioned razor over a foot long. It was said that when he was alone in the dorm, he made two cuts in his inguinal artery, one cut in his abdomen to lift out the intestines, two cuts to his wrists, two cuts on his arms, and one cut in his throat, so as to leave no chance of survival. His blood spurted out from the deep wounds onto the wall by the bed. The quilt that covered his body was seeped in blood. Drained of blood, his body shriveled to a mere shadow of itself.

It was the fall of 1970 when Zhang Xiaoxiao, Yao Yao's childhood friend, together with her newlywed husband, went to Yao Yao's home to visit her. The raging storm of the Red Guard Movement had been replaced by the "To the Hills and the Villages" Campaign. Batches of Shanghai youth were sent to villages in the North. The drums and gongs moving down the streets were in celebration of their departure to be re-educated by the poor and lower-middle peasants. The fierce clamor of the drums and gongs accentuated the increasing silence of the city. Like a middle-aged person collapsing after strenuous exercises, the city suddenly grew old that summer after experiencing the heat of raging flames and red flags. The white glare of street lamps revealed black stains on the walls around the decaying water pipes of the houses, which were in a sad state of disrepair. The untrimmed sycamore branches were entwined overhead. The red paint on the walls had lost its luster. When walking up the stairs of the building where Yao Yao lived, Zhang Xiaoxiao noticed that the big-character posters covering the hallway had been scraped off, leaving faint ink stains on the wainscot panels. All was quiet in the hallway. Everyone had long gone to bed.

It was a stranger who answered the door for Zhang Xiaoxiao. There were now three families living in Shangguan Yunzhu's apartment.

"Yao Yao looked very surprised when she saw us," said Zhang Xiaoxiao. "She was wearing a brown woolen jacket. Her hair was gathered up in a bun on the top of her head. She was very thin."

Dengdeng said, "My sister gathered up her long hair into a top bun in order to hide a lock of white hair at the top of her head. It had turned white on the day she learned about Yan Kai's death."

In Yao Yao's room remained a round, carved mahogany table. It was covered with a sheet of newspaper on which were laid some air-dried noodles, the kind that were available every morning in Shanghai's grain stores. They were freshly made and sold at 0.17 yuan a catty. Made from standard whole wheat flour, they were dark in color and, once cooked, would make the water turn green because of all the alkaline in them. One could also buy noodles, made of refined white flour, at 0.21 yuan a catty. It was the former variety that Yao Yao was air-drying. She had rolled up the fresh noodles into small balls, spread them out on newspapers and air-dried them. She could have bought dried noodles, but they cost 0.31 yuan a catty and took longer to cook *al dente*. She ate one ball for each meal. After Shangguan's death, Yao Yao's only income was the thirty yuan provided by her stepfather.

"Why don't you come eat with us and have whatever we have?" said Zhang Xiaoxiao to her. She gave Yao Yao her new address.

I asked Zhang Xiaoxiao, "Did she cry?"

"No. She looked absent-minded, as if her thoughts were elsewhere. I did not say a word about Yan Kai. I felt so sorry for her. But I did ask her why she wasn't living with her mother when she died. I honestly could not understand why. She gave me a look as I asked, as if there was something she could not bring herself to say. Finally she said that she had been very busy at the Conservatory. Later, the old maidservant told me that for a time, Yao Yao had so much ardor for the revolution that she hated going home. As for me, I would rather die than sever ties with my parents."

"And she didn't mention Yan Kai either?" I asked.

"No," said Zhang Xiaoxiao.

From that time on, Yao Yao went to Zhang Xiaoxiao's home on Yanqing Road almost every day. Later she managed to find Cheng Shuyao, who had been expelled from his former residence and was now living on Wuyuan Road. From Zhang Xiaoxiao's home, she often went on to see Cheng Shuyao. There was a small red-brick Christian church on the way along that road. The stained glass windows of the church had been smashed at the beginning of the Cultural Revolution, and the church stood in ruins, but the notes of an organ still often wafted out of the classroom of an elementary school next to the church. It was a revolutionary music class. The antiquated wooden organ sounded as if it was sobbing even when it was playing the happiest music. Wuyuan Road was in fact a narrow street that was permeated with the air of simple and honest everyday life. Even in 1971, the former owner of Lili Flowers in Wuyuan Road Food Market was still selling fresh roses. Since her shop had closed, she put her flowers in a shallow bamboo basket and walked as she hawked her ware. In summer, she sold white magnolia buds by the roadside amid the sweet aroma of the flowers mixed with the rank smell of the open-air fish stands. "Gardenia! White magnolia buds!" she cried. Along the street stood new-style row houses with steel-sash windows, behind which hung white curtains made out of mosquito nets. The eateries with their square tables and benches had large kegs of draft beer for sale. In summer, children on errands bought beer with thermo bottles for their parents, for only the price of a catty of noodles. The peaceful life palpable on Wuyuan Road must have brought solace to Yao Yao's heart. Walking day after day on this alley with its aura of blissful domestic life, Yao Yao gradually began to smile again. "Dad!" she still called Cheng Shuyao in her girlish way. There, she made Shanghai-style potato salad with Wu Yan. They diced boiled potatoes, peeled and diced sausages and tossed them with sweet fresh peas and a peeled and diced apple. They added salad oil to an egg yolk, stirred the mixture with chopsticks until it gained the right consistency, and poured the dressing over all the ingredients. This was an indispensable Western-style side dish served at big parties in the families that lived on Wuyuan Road in the 1970s. Sometimes, when Yao Yao was already on her way out of the building, Cheng Shuyao would run after her and shout, "*Baobei*, come again tomorrow! We'll make potato salad!"

Cheng Shuyao and his third wife Wu Yan occupied a room on the second floor. He had become a man able to take any insults without getting angry and remain content as long as pork chops were available at the meat stall in the neighborhood. In his black-rimmed glasses and his darned khaki pants, he sat on a carved tall-back teak chair and amused himself by translating Shakespeare's comedies. The tapestry of the chair was so dirty and old that in the rainy season of June, it emitted a combination of odors, and the Victorian-style carvings were covered with dust. Sitting in such a chair, Cheng Shuyao did not wax nostalgic and mournful, as one would have expected of him. Instead, he accepted the adversities in his life with a mildly cheerful frame of mind. His schoolmate at Yenching University, Huang Zongjiang, said, "He not only accepted adversity, he practically embraced it with enthusiasm. That's why he was always cheerful."

In 1949, on the eve of the liberation of Shanghai, the members of the underground Communist Party led by Pan Hannian talked a large number of well-known figures of Shanghai into staying in Shanghai to welcome the Liberation. The social butterfly "Linghua Number 9" rendered outstanding service in the endeavor. In 1949, this celebrated courtesan donned a coarse-cloth uniform and became a government official, as arranged by Pan Hannian himself. Only then did she resume her real name Wu Yan, a name she had not used since she entered a brothel at age fourteen. In 1955, she was sent to Tilanqiao Prison because of her involvement in Pan Hannian's case. On the same day, all her property was confiscated, and her house in Hongqiao, with its huge garden and its orchard, was sealed up. Her marriage with Cheng Shuyao was only into its first year. She did not return to Cheng Shuyao's home until the eve of the Cultural Revolution. When Dengdeng went from Beijing to spend his summer vacation in Shanghai, Yao Yao came to see her brother and felt drawn to Wu Yan. With her spoiled-girl ways with Cheng Shuyao, Yao Yao brought joy to Cheng Shuyuao and Wu Yan in their dull life in that small and old grey house. Just as when Yao Yao was nine years old, nothing sensitive was said in her hearing, as if no horrible thing had ever happened all those years.

For a time, Yao Yao learned Beijing opera from Wu Yan, who had acquired the art in her days at the pleasure quarters. She played older male roles (*laosheng*). Later, Zhang Boju, the only true remaining disciple of Yu Shuyan, taught Wu Yan all the famous arias in Yu Shuyan's repertoirc. Wu Yan's wide social network included Bao Jixiang and Li Shaochun, who had both taught her; Meng Xiaodong, who was a very close friend of hers; and Mei Lanfang, whose younger son Mei Baojiu was her godson. At the fund-raising event hosted by Cheng Shuyao to honor the troops upon the Liberation of Shanghai, Wu Yan went on the stage with the famous Mei Lanfang and Zhou Xinfang in a major role. She taught Yao Yao to sing Li Tiemei's arias from the modern play *The Red Lantern* in the traditional way, bringing out the cadences in ancient Chinese.

And so, residents on Wuyuan Road often heard Yao Yao's singing.

One fine day, a man went to visit his relatives on the first floor and, quite by chance, found out that his old friend Cheng Shuyao, whom he hadn't heard from in a long time, was living upstairs. So he went up to seek Cheng out. As Cheng opened the door, standing against the window and blocking the light, both men's forlorn, subdued, docile but alert and resentful faces broke into smiles, like gaping wounds oozing blood. The visitor sidled in and the door was closed. Later, he took his wife's daughter and his concubine's son for another visit to Cheng Shuyao. His concubine had gone to the US and landed a job at the United Nations in the Chinese Translation Service. Sitting on Cheng Shuyao's tall-backed chair with frayed satin upholstery, he recited passages from *Hamlet*, a play that he had acted in when he was young, and melted in tears.

That day, in the greenish sunlight that filtered through the bamboo curtain, Yao Yao met the teenager Kaikai, who bore a strong resemblance to Yan Kai.

It was the summer of 1971. She was 27, a young woman who had no parents, no home, no lover, no diploma, and no job. But as long as she was there, the whole room echoed with her laughter and singing. They played bridge together and, with doors and windows tightly shut, listened to Kaikai's collection of records. The gramophone needle, when tracing the fine grooves on the black records, like train wheels running on railway tracks, brought out the music hidden in them. They also talked about books they had read. Yao Yao had no interest in Chinese classics but was drawn to 19th century European novels like Tolstoy's *Resurrection* and Goethe's *The Sorrows of Young Werther*. She sang "Ode to Beijing" with the passion of Violetta in *La Traviata*. Kaikai had not yet graduated from high school but was quite well-read and much given to volunteering commentaries on books. Yao Yao would quiet down only when she was alone but then, she would become a rock that, laden with grief, hurtled helplessly into the bottom of a bitter sea. As she cast her eyes down, Kaikai would stay behind and stand by her. He called her "Older Sister Yao Yao."

More daring but also more cautious than Yan

Kai, Kaikai had a secret channel of communication with his birth mother in New York, and was applying for a passport so as to be reunited with her in New York. His mother helped Yao Yao find her birth father Yao Ke, who was living in Hawaii. Yao Ke had relocated there from Hong Kong in 1968 after getting a position as a visiting professor in a university in Hawaii. Yao Yao wrote a letter to him and Kaikai had it brought to America by different hands through a circuitous route. In those days, the US being China's worst enemy, there were no diplomatic relations between the two countries and therefore, no reciprocal shipping or postal services. American-educated people were not trusted, even if they had returned to China decades earlier. Those who listened to the Voice of America could be labeled counter-revolutionaries if found out. Shanghai intellectuals transliterated the word "English" as "into the gutters" in the Shanghai dialect.

On December 7, 1972, as a requirement for job assignment, graduates of the Vocal Music Department were told to take a physical exam at the Xuhui District Medical Center. Late for her appointment, Zhong

Wan found the hospital quite empty. In the lobby, she ran into Yao Yao on her way out of a doctor's office, her face flaming red. Zhong Wan called after her, but she pushed on with a perfunctory word of greeting. As Zhong Wan poked her head into the office, the doctor stopped her and told her to immediately notify the Conservatory that Yao Yao was seven months pregnant.

"I ran out after Yao Yao, but she was already out of sight," said Zhong Wan. "So I immediately went to the Conservatory and warned the Workers' Propaganda Team that something might happen to Yao Yao. They told me to find her as soon possible. It was the first time I went to Yao Yao's home. He Lu, her stepfather, said to me icily that he had no idea where she was. The next morning, the school janitor gave me a telephone message from Yao Yao, telling me not to look for her, because she had already left Shanghai."

"What do you mean by 'something might happen to her'?" I asked.

"I was afraid that she might take it too hard and do something to herself, because an out-of-the-wedlock pregnancy in those days was a major scandal.

A few weeks later, I saw Yao Yao being escorted under guard through the entrance gate, her pregnancy showing through her cotton-padded full-length coat. She kept her eyes down and didn't look at anyone."

The day after the physical exam, Yao Yao and Kaikai fled to Guangzhou. They wanted to continue on to Shenzhen, which was then a small deserted fishing village with tall wire nets all along the riverbank. Due to its proximity to the border, railway stations demanded to see special letters of permission when selling tickets to Shenzhen. They did bring an official letter from an unsuspecting neighbor, but it didn't work. Yao Yao wrote in her confession to school authorities, "At our wits' end, we walked back and forth in the railway station. Witnessing overseas Chinese and compatriots from Hong Kong and Macao greeting their loved ones at the station, we missed our loved ones even more. We sat on the slope of a hill by the Sha River and watched trains coming and going for hours without being able to figure out a way to go to Shenzhen. When a freight train went by, loaded with hogs, Kaikai hit on the idea of hiding in a freight train to Hong Kong. He said he wanted to give it a try. After we agreed on meeting the next day in the hotel, he left for the railway station."

Kaikai did not return the next day, nor the third day. While Yao Yao was waiting anxiously in their hotel room, Kaikai had been captured by border guards. Because Yao Yao was not guilty of defection and was pregnant, she was allowed to be taken back to the Conservatory. By this time, Yao Yao didn't have enough money left for a train ticket to Shanghai. It was a relative of hers who resignedly paid the Conservatory.

Zhong Wan said, "One day, I was standing behind her in a line in the school cafeteria when I said to her softly, 'How could you have been such a fool!' She said, looking down, 'It was all my fault. I am to blame. I brought him to this pass.'"

"Why didn't Yao Yao go home?" I asked. I wondered how she could cope with the school environment in her physical condition.

"How could she? She was not allowed to go home. Her case was still under investigation. What she had done could have landed her in jail in those days. She got herself pregnant. Remember the historical context! Yao Yao had done enough to bring

disgrace and ruin on herself!" said Zhong Wan to me
in a reproachful tone softened with a smile.

"How did she manage to survive?" I asked.
Shangguan Yunzhu and Yan Kai, those dearest and
nearest to her, had committed suicide, but not Yao
Yao. In her own words, "When I did a grievous wrong
and was in the greatest danger, it was the school
authorities who rescued me." It was January 4, 1973,
thirteen days before her due date.

"Did she wash herself in the women's bathhouse
at the Conservatory?"

"Where else? It was deep winter, but there was
no heating, nor hot water anywhere else."

"Did you see her bathe herself? I mean, did you
accompany her?" I asked.

Zhong Wan shook her head. "In those days,
nobody had time for other people. If something
happened to you, people around you would cut you
dead, as if you had become a stranger to them overnight. But they didn't look at you the way strangers
did. Strangers wouldn't look as though they were
going to watch you die without lifting a finger to help
you. She lived alone in the school where nobody talked

to her. She was seen from a distance and denounced at meetings, large and small, in awful rhetoric. Even her mother's way of life was used against her. She stayed there until she was hospitalized for delivery."

Soon thereafter, Zhong Wan asked to be assigned to the Song and Dance Ensemble of Jilin Province and left Shanghai.

On January 17, 1973, Yao Yao quietly gave birth to a baby boy in a yellow-walled delivery room amid the screams of pain of other women in labor. The obstetrician who delivered the baby for Yao Yao said, "She didn't cry out in pain. She was very quiet." The doctor had a gentle but sad face, with deep-set eyes. Her hands resting on the table looked like the hands of just another elderly woman, but those were hands that had delivered thousands of babies.

"Generally speaking, such women know their place and have greater tolerance for pain," said a nurse who worked there at the time.

"As doctors, our job is to help the women deliver babies. We don't care about what they had done previously in their lives," said the doctor. "When she was admitted, someone came to put in a word for her, telling me that she was Shangguan Yunzhu's daughter. I knew her mother had died. Our society being topsyturvy at the time, I thought there must have been a reason why she had gotten into such a mess."

I believe that the one who put in a word for Yao Yao must have been her nurse, who had been a midwife before she started working for Shangguan Yunzhu.

"How did Yao Yao look?" I asked.

"She was taller and bigger than her mother but not as pretty. But at first glance, I still saw the resemblance. She looked like a model." After so many years and so many deliveries, the doctor still remembered her looks.

"Did she look heartbroken?" I asked.

"No. She looked peaceful, normal, and tough. I didn't see anything unusual about her," said the doctor.

Was this due to Yao Yao's pretenses or her strong willpower? Like her mother, even if she wanted to indulge in tears, she would not tell others why she did so.

After giving birth, Yao Yao was transferred to a large six-bed ward.

"My bed was right opposite hers. I first saw the pair of brown leather boots under her bed. In those days, very few women got to wear such beautiful boots. I could tell by the way she carried herself that she was from a family of high culture. She looked a lot like her mother. Later, I heard a nurse say in the lavatory that she didn't want the baby. The father was many years younger than she was. It wasn't a regular marriage." Quite by chance, I found a woman who happened to have shared the same ward with Yao Yao. She was a simple, decent woman with a soft and tolerant expression of empathy on her face.

I learned that an elderly woman and a man had visited Yao Yao. My guess is that the elderly woman was her childhood nurse. But who was that man? After Yao Yao's scandal came to light, Cheng Shuyao cut all ties with her and declared that he would never have anything to do with her again. Kaikai was in detention, and his father had also broken off relations with the Cheng family, believing that it was the immoral Yao Yao who had seduced young Kaikai and brought Kaikai to such a pass. So Kaikai's family could not have visited her, either. The identity of that man remains a mystery to this day. When Mrs. Sun, the nurse, walked up to Yao Yao's bed, did she call her "*Baobei*," the nickname that stuck with Yao Yao since her birth?

"What did she do when her ward-mates had visitors and she had none?" I asked.

"She seemed to have just closed her eyes for a rest."

"She just closed her eyes?"

The ward-mate gave my question some thought and smiled apologetically. "Actually, I didn't quite notice. I was too involved in talking with my husband to really notice. Every day we breast-fed three times. In those days, mothers and babies were kept apart, in separate wards. So each time, the nurses carried the babies out to the mothers, with the one exception of *her* baby."

The elderly nurse said, "If a baby is to be adopted, we don't want to take the baby to its mother, because at the sight of the baby, the mother might change her mind and refuse to give it away. It's her flesh and blood, after all. Once she gets to look at the baby, she would hate to part with it. But in Yao Yao's case, on the day after the delivery, no clear instructions were left when the nurses changed shift, so her baby was taken to her. I heard her say immediately to the nurse, 'I'm not going to feed him.' She gave the baby back to the nurse at once."

"Did she hug him?" I asked. Imagine, her own baby in front of her! A pink and sweet-smelling little baby!

"No. She gave him back to the nurse at once."

"She didn't even give him one little hug?"

"No," she replied, giving me a look. "I thought that she had a heart of stone, treating her own baby like that."

Zhang Xiaoxiao said, "That day, Yao Yao told me that she kept talking and laughing until evening, but she spent the whole night weeping under her quilt."

"She must have been a very unusual person in the ward, and everybody knew what she had done," I said. "Did anyone ask her questions?"

"No. Why bring up something that would only hurt her? No one asked anything," she replied.

It may never have occurred to Yao Yao that the obstetric ward would turn out to be a place most embarrassing for her, where she would have felt loneliest and the most vulnerable. However, her ward-mates, women whom she had never seen before and who, like that worker from a radio factory, do not know her name even to this day, protected her self-respect with their silence. They gave nothing away, so Yao Yao thought that they knew nothing. In fact, they all knew but chose to keep their lips sealed so that she could enjoy some peace and quiet.

On the day she was discharged from the hospital, the head nurse called her to the hallway and asked her for the last time if she wanted to take the baby with her or not. She said no and wrote a pledge, promising never to claim the baby back. The baby was adopted by a married couple, both doctors. They gave Yao Yao 200 yuan for her to buy nutritious food with, and promised to take good care of the baby.

The ward-mate continued, "That day, she left the hospital by herself. I don't think anyone came to pick her up. She went downstairs all alone to settle the bill. She first came to my bedside and said, 'I'm leaving.' I said goodbye to her. She didn't take the baby, and went off all alone. She must have felt bad. She said goodbye in a very low voice, and left just like that."

And so she left the ward on the 5th floor. The

freshly mopped wet floor of the hallway shone with the reflection of the yellow doors of the wards. It was morning, at the hour when the babies were to be taken out of the babies' room. Some impatient mothers, in their blue-and-white striped gowns, waited in the hallway for the wooden cribs to emerge. Like little chicks in a basket in spring, the babies lying in the spacious cribs made all sorts of noises, each crying in its own way. The sweet, lovely sounds spreading from the end of the hallway to the obstetrics ward were the sounds of paradise for the mothers. Even those lying in bed would instantly sit up and lift their clothes, whether or not they had enough milk for breast-feeding at that moment.

The walls had Chairman Mao's quotations posted on them. Written in red on thick drawing paper were these words: "Be resolute. Fear no sacrifice, and surmount every difficulty to win victory." In those days, this was a popular quotation for display on hospital walls. Yao Yao walked past the quotations down the stairs.

She returned home and slept in her mother's bed. Opposite her small bed was her stepfather's bed. The layout was the same as before Shangguan Yunzhu's death. He Lu was working in the countryside and rarely returned to Shanghai on leave, but all of a sudden, Yao Yao began to seek accommodation with friends. She adamantly refused to sleep under the same roof with her stepfather when he was home.

Dengdeng said, "I think something must have happened between them. He Lu became her stepfather when she was only seven, but she always called him Uncle He Lu. They didn't get along. But she never told me what had happened, if anything. Maybe it was because I lived so far away in Shanxi Province. Maybe she couldn't bring herself to confide in a little brother."

Zhang Xiaoxiao said, "Yao Yao told me that her stepfather was working at the May 7th Cadres' School in the countryside and rarely came on leave to Shanghai. Whenever he did, she felt so uncomfortable that she often had to spend the night in the bathroom. So she had no place to call her own."

As the graduating students were being assigned jobs, Yao Yao's dorm entitlements had been terminated. Zhong Wan had already gone to Jilin

Province, and Zhang Xiaoxiao had only a 6-square-meter room to call home. Henceforth, Yao Yao never went out without a large black bag in which she kept her most important items. But she never moved the small bed that belonged to her. She kept it the way it had been before Shangguan Yunzhu's death. Nor did she use pieces of furniture to divide the large room into two, as was a common practice in Shanghai. With the acute housing shortage in Shanghai, some families also used fiber boards to serve as dividers, but Yao Yao kept the room intact. When taking photographs, she would make a point of sitting by the carved end-table that her mother had liked, and her face would still wear a smile.

Dengdeng wrote his father Cheng Shuyao several letters in a row, asking him to bring his sister into the Cheng household. So one day, Yao Yao followed Cheng Shuyao home and spent the night on the couch, since there was no space for an extra bed in that one-room home. Yao Yao could not very well stay there long.

"Do you know that Dengdeng's uncle Cheng Shuming had committed suicide?" said Zhang Xiaoxiao.

"The Workers' Propaganda Team of his work unit wanted to put him under detention. They made him carry his own baggage when escorting him out of his home. He couldn't take the insult and killed himself. Yao Yao told me that Dengdeng was badly shaken."

Dengdeng denied this. "No, if I had a violent reaction I don't remember it. Didn't my mother commit suicide? Didn't Yan Kai, whom I had always considered my brother-in-law, also commit suicide? I would have been prepared for this."

Perhaps Yao Yao's words about Dengdeng being badly shaken were a clue to her own feelings.

Someone told me, "If I had been Yao Yao, I would have killed myself long ago. If I had been reduced to such a sorry state and if my mother had died, why would I, the orphan, hang on to life? Wouldn't death have solved everything?"

But Yao Yao did not choose to die. In a photograph taken at that time, she was sitting on a green lawn on a summer day, her hands clasping her knees, her lips parted in a smile as big as a white magnolia blossom that no one could stop from blooming.

One day, she went with a childhood friend to see

a Ms. Shang who owned a piano, because she wanted to find a piano to practice her singing in preparation for graduation. Ms. Shang had come to Shanghai as a member of the art troupe of the Third Field Army of the People's Liberation Army, and right after Liberation, had played the title role on stage in the play *The White Haired Girl*.

"So you are Yao Yao?" exclaimed Auntie Shang. "When you and your mother came to watch our rehearsal, you were only this tall, with a huge bow on your head." Auntie Shang recalled those words to me, gesturing. "Yao Yao laughed and said, 'Yes, that's true.'

"That day, she said she had no place to stay for the night. So she stayed with us. Later, when she gradually confided in me what she had gone through, my heart went out to her. I told her to move in at once to live with my family. She was exhilarated and did move in. Sadly, it wasn't so much 'moving' as just bringing her few clothes over.

"I still vividly remember Yao Yao. In her girlish way, she often rubbed her cheek against my shoulder, the way a little dog does, saying, 'Auntie, Auntie.' I really felt sorry for that girl." Her face lit by the dreamy, distracted smile of a mother responding to the display of affection of her pampered child, Auntie Shang tapped her own shoulder to show me where Yao Yao had rubbed her face. "After she moved in, I noticed she was really hard up and was penny pinching. Even though she had no expenses living with my family, a girl that age should have some money on her. Her stepfather used to give her 20 yuan a month, but later changed his mind. I showed her the drawer where we put money. In those days we didn't have much money, and the drawer was never locked. I told her to feel free to help herself to it, as my daughter did. But Yao Yao hardly ever did. Whenever she was desperate for money, she would tell me in advance about her need for it, looking very embarrassed. She was indeed a very mature and sensible child." So saying, Auntie Shang gradually hid her face behind her two hands so as to block it from view. A vein traveled through the thin back of her hand like a river on a map. "It hurts me to think of that girl. As they say, one misstep results in eternal regret. Everything that happened then was driving her into a corner. I feel sad beyond words whenever I think of her."

Auntie Shang's eyes, framed by tiny wrinkles, reddened as they welled up with tears. She shut her eyes tightly, like a child being forced by the Phys Ed teacher to jump off the diving board into the deep end of the pool. I was overwhelmed with apologetic feelings for having triggered some deeply-buried memories. I saw in my mind's eye the mournful faces of my former interviewees at the mention of traumatic events in their lives. I little know when and how to raise questions so as not to disturb the quiet lives they enjoy now. Puckering up her face in painful memory, Auntie Shang continued, "But I do often think of her. Sometimes, she just pops up before my eyes."

So Yao Yao finally had a place to stay. It was already the summer of 1973. The green mosquito-repelling incense that Auntie Shang used emitted a smell and a grayish vapor that gave comfort to those afraid of mosquitoes. Lying on a rattan deckchair, Yao Yao must have seemed like a large piece of luggage that had finally arrived at its destination after being transferred from station to station. Did she have a sense of security amid the vapor of the incense?

A friend of hers told me, "She was a frightened girl.

Once when I accompanied her home, we were walking up the stairs when we heard police sirens downstairs. She was greatly alarmed and pushed me away, telling me to leave at once. She stood still by herself in the dark hallway, as if wondering if the police car would stop right there. It wasn't until the police siren subsided and the police car had gone far that she calmed down." It was the very same hallway that had been covered with posters denouncing her mother in 1968, that had witnessed her travails in the summer of 1970 when she felt as good as dead, and that she had passed through that morning in 1972 when, seven months pregnant, she left home with only enough money to buy a one-way train ticket, intending to sneak across the border. When she stood in the dark hallway that night, listening to the police siren whizzing by, her mother had died, her son had been given away for adoption, and her former boyfriend was still in jail. All these were events that would have constituted entries in her disgraceful personal dossier.

In 1972, job assignments for college graduates finally got off to a start in Shanghai. Due to the Cultural Revolution, five consecutive graduating classes of college students stayed behind on campus. The job assignments were decided by the Workers' Propaganda Teams on the various campuses. Before her scandal broke out, Yao Yao had been put on the list of candidates for the choir affiliated with the Shanghai Symphony Orchestra, at a time when the orchestra and the choir were rehearsing the revolutionary Beijing opera *Sha Jia Village*. But after Yao Yao was found to be pregnant, the Workers Propaganda Team cancelled their plan and decided to send her to Yellow Mountains Farm in Anhui Province. The Job Assignment Team told her that her personal dossier, which included records of her family background and her own behavior, was so disgraceful that no work unit in Shanghai's music industry would be willing to accept her. They added that there would be too much resentment if someone like her could get to stay in Shanghai.

A man who was in the powerful position of assigning jobs to the graduating class of another college told me, "In those days, assigning someone to such a place was a punishment. Those who misbehaved had to pay a price. That was the rule. And hers was such a bad case, too. If the college were to assign *one* person to far-flung Gansu Province, that person would have to be her. Haggling over it was out of the question."

"Would that be fair?" I asked.

"It was fair according to the standards of those days. If your personal dossier was that bad, you just had to swallow the punishment."

On the dining table by the balcony of Auntie Shang's apartment, Yao Yao had written the following words: "I have indeed done wrong things in the past, but the more the school authorities use them as a trump card to force me to leave Shanghai, the more I hate to be pushed out as a punishment, and to be accused of making 'mistakes' and causing 'resentment.' My stepfather would be more than happy to use these accusations to justify his moves to drive me out. This is not the right thing to do. (Of course I am wise enough to know that you can't always expect to find justice in this world.) I must atone for my past mistakes by my actions, and fight them forcefully but flexibly, to show them in the end who I really am. I still trust that there is a truth to everything. There are rights and wrongs. I didn't do right by my mother and my son, but I will not allow such people to continue to bully me, insult me, and misrepresent me, because by doing so, they are insulting my mother and my flesh and blood. I just want to win some honor for myself."

So, for the first time, Yao Yao defied the school authorities: She adamantly refused to go to Yellow Mountains Farm. The school authorities shelved her case and went on to other students.

The man who had been in a position of power told me, "If someone in our college dared to do this, I would have given him or her the same treatment. It was in fact a smart move—putting the case aside. If the college did not assign you a job, your personal dossier would have no place to go to, and you are at a dead end, because you wouldn't have a job, a salary, or a residency permit. When festivals approached, the neighborhood committees might even kick those without residency permits out of Shanghai. The residency system in those days was very strict, nothing like what we have now. Most people couldn't tough it out and had to go where they were assigned. So we didn't have to get angry. We needed only to shelve the case and wait for them to come around and ask for forgiveness." So saying, the man broke into a cruel smile, becoming a completely different man from the gentle and affable man I first came to know. He, also, was immersed in memories of the past. In a moment, he came to himself and said with a laugh, "But that was a long time ago."

Yao Yao went to the Conservatory every day, following Auntie Shang's advice, partly to show the public that she was obeying the rules and never missed a day at the Conservatory, and partly to remind the Workers' Propaganda Team that their job was not yet complete. Every day she heard news about her schoolmates leaving campus to take up their jobs. Every day, she went to see members of the Workers' Propaganda Team, only to be cold-shouldered. With an ingratiating smile, she pleaded her case over and over again, and they rejected her over and over again, telling her that no work unit was willing to accept her dossier. "They didn't even deign to look at me, as if I was trash," said Yao Yao to Auntie Shang upon returning home. Auntie Shang told me, "I always comforted her by telling her to hold her ground. If there's a will, there's a way."

Soon the job-assignment team of the Conservatory told Yao Yao to go to Hunan Province, declaring that they would never assign her a job in Shanghai. This time, they handed her an official letter addressed to the work unit in Hunan as well as the notification of her departure from the Conservatory, and told her to terminate her relationship with the Conservatory. Again Yao Yao refused. The Workers' Propaganda Team told Yao Yao in irritation that if she wanted a job at all, Hunan it was! The Conservatory was not going to give her a re-assignment.

Xia Zhongyi said, "So she must have also heard the phrase 'this winter or next spring,' a phrase that began to catch on in the summer of 1973. At that time, all those awaiting job assignment knew the hidden meaning of that catchphrase. It meant that what did not materialize for us in the summer might arrive in winter or in spring of next year. It may have first appeared in a newspaper editorial or one of the Central Party Committee's documents, but later evolved into a phrase associated with waiting and hoping. There was another catchphrase that said, 'You can find where your comrades are by singing *The Internationale*.' 'This winter or next spring' meant the same thing for us as *The Internationale* means for revolutionaries."

"Wasn't that an expression of despair?" I asked, puzzled.

He replied, "In those days, there was no freedom of choice. If the government didn't give you a job, you had no way out. So everybody expected the government to give us something, to adopt a new policy, to read us new instructions from a Central Party Committee document—in short, to bring us improvements in life. So, that phrase 'this winter or next spring' was an expression not of despair, but of hope."

"But wouldn't someone silently hoping for something to turn up resemble a frog trying over and over again to jump out of a deep well?" I asked him.

Zhang Xiaoxiao said, "At that time, I heard that some people were trying to make a match for Yao Yao, because in her case, they thought it might be better for her to marry and settle down before planning the next thing to do. Yao Yao often came to see me, and a friend of mine, a fine painter, had his eyes on Yao Yao. Auntie Shang was also worried about her. I believe she had also been on the lookout for possible candidates. So had Wu Yan. They were all afraid that if she drifted along like that, something would happen to her again.

And she was in too much agony."

However, nothing came of their efforts.

One fine afternoon on a summer's day in Shanghai, in the greenish sunlight filtering through the bamboo curtain in a second-floor room, where Yao Yao had come to know Kaikai a few years before, Wu Yan introduced Yao Yao to a relative of Cheng Shuyao's. She kept the two of them for dinner. In the communal kitchen on the ground floor, she put a bowl of salad and the candied pork shoulder she had cooked onto a wooden tray and carried it upstairs, her hair smelling of grease. The wooden stairs were in a poor state of repair and creaked as she went up. I found it hard to believe that this was the celebrity who had won a lawsuit against Dai Li, head of the Nationalist Party's spy agency, over ownership of an estate in Suzhou. Yao Yao had gone down and made fried banana, the way her mother had taught her.

Placing the candied pork shoulder in the middle of the table, Wu Yan said, "I hope you will soon treat me to your version of a pork shoulder (A cooked pork shoulder is a gift for a matchmaker in the Shanghai tradition)." Yao Yao lowered her head and gave a smile without saying anything.

According to Dengdeng, in the 1950s, in some distinguished families overthrown by the revolution, the concubines and the daughters, with nowhere to turn to for help, quietly married themselves off to trustworthy men, to shake themselves free of the marks of their social class and settle for a simple but peaceful life. Some of Wu Yan's old friends had done so.

In Yao Yao's case, if she couldn't find a job, at least she should have someone to depend on for financial support. I believe this was a legitimate concern. This was reality, undisguised. Even if Wu Yan hadn't said it out loud, Yao Yao would have gotten her point. Through her own experience, Yao Yao must also have come to appreciate Wu Yan's feelings. Having gone through so much in life, Wu Yan had abandoned all dreams by now but was full of the courage to live on tenaciously, however great the injustices done to her.

"What was that man's name?" asked Zhang Xiaoxiao.

"Cheng Yuxian," I told her.

"Once, I ran into Yao Yao and him on the street. He looked like a simple and honest man. Nothing extraordinary about him. He had on a pair of beige khaki pants. Yao Yao said that he was quite devoted to her and was very nice to her, but that they were not the same kind of people. She couldn't love him."

I did not expect to hear that Yao Yao was still talking seriously about love at a time like that. So her passion for love, which everybody thought had died out, was still growing in her, like the flourishing wild lilies in a deserted marsh that catch intruders by surprise.

"What kind of a person do you think Yao Yao was?" I asked.

Cheng Yuxian replied, "She was an innocent girl. An unsophisticated girl."

"She had gone through so much in her life, and you still think she was an innocent girl?"

"I still do."

Zhang Xiaoxiao said, "Yao Yao was really a sad case. She had no way out at that time."

During that period, was there absolutely nothing to cheer her up?

Zhang Xiaoxiao said, "Yes, there was something. One day, she came and showed me a letter from Yao

Ke, written with a brush pen on a piece of rice paper. So her father had written to accept her as his daughter! Years ago, Kaikai had asked his mother to deliver letters from Yao Yao to him, but he never replied. Now that the reply had come after such a long interval, Yao Yao was wild with joy. She was already almost thirty. When she was feeling low, she looked older, but that day, her big smile took years off her age. She was really happy that day. Her father said that there were three possible places where they could meet: Shanghai, but he was being denounced by Chairman Mao, so he couldn't very well return to Shanghai without courting death. And then there were Hong Kong and the United States. If Yao Yao could be allowed to leave the mainland, he could go to Hong Kong to see her, or have her fly to America. She gave me the scare of my life. In those days, such a letter would have landed her in prison. It was a case of 'having illicit relations with a foreign country.' That was a major crime, and Yao Yao would be a 'repeat offender.' I asked her what she was going to do about the letter. She said she would carry it on her at all times. I knew she would never burn it, so I just told her to hide it well."

Auntie Shang said, "Yao Yao told me something about it. She said that her folks in Suzhou had found where Yao Ke was. I was so frightened I grabbed her hands and said, 'Don't you ever get involved in such things again! You can't afford to do the wrong thing again.' I knew she missed her father but, at that stage of her life, she just couldn't let something happen to her again. She promised me and said, OK, Auntie. But she said that just to stop my worries."

That day, she told Zhang Xiaoxiao about an incident in her childhood when she was six or seven: She had a grudge against her mother and ran away from home, taking a small bag with her. A police officer on the street took her into his booth and had her mother go and claim her back. Why did she suddenly recall that incident?

Yao Yao decided that it would be better if she could find a good job on her own.

Auntie Shang said, "In those days, you were not supposed to look for jobs on your own. Everything you did had to be approved by the authorities. Jobs were *assigned* to you. What I could help Yao Yao do was to go with her to seek out people in a position to talk to those in power at the Conservatory, and ask them to talk to the job-assignment team into reopening Yao Yao's case and giving her a job. We in the army have no idea how to give gifts and how to play up to people. I was advised to present gifts to those I was asking favors of, but I really didn't know how to do it. I was so embarrassed. I would take a large bottle of cooking oil, a bag of dried mushroom or other stuff not easily available at the time, and sometimes some apples, and go knocking on doors, with Yao Yao in tow. As soon as I was let in, I would put the gifts by the door and be done with it."

"You must have felt bad to stoop so low," I said.

"Of course! My children all joined the army, to serve under my old comrades-in-arms, so I didn't have to do that sort of thing. But Yao Yao was different. What choice did she have? But all the trouble we took came to nothing. They always said, 'It can't be done. If Yao Yao were to stay in Shanghai, there would be too much resentment.' Some people gave their promises to my face, but in fact did nothing. When I went to them again a few days later, they would say, 'Why don't we wait for a good opportunity to turn up?' Actually they had no intention to help in the first place. They just didn't want to have anything to do with Yao Yao, so as not to be implicated in any way. Goodness knows how many walls we ran into, some harder than others. Yao Yao was in a lot of agony. Sometimes I saw her sitting in the rattan chair on the balcony, looking disturbed, although she said nothing. I did tell her not to worry, but not having a job was not the way to go."

Finally, Yao Yao herself began to lose hope. It was as if she was standing on quicksand. So even though she had her feet firmly on it, she still could not keep herself from wobbling. She began to realize that an ideal job was beyond her reach. She had said in frustration, "For everyone in the world, preconceived ideas take a strong hold. However hard I try, the moment they see my file and hear about what I have done, they turn against me and won't take me on." But she still kept her feet on the sand.

Her dossier seemed like a sharp sword that held her at bay and kept her head down. Everybody believed that her file contained much that was unfavorable to her. When I was sitting in front of that mysterious large brown paper envelope containing her dossier, I also thought of it as the weapon that undid her. The envelope gave off the smell of dust, and particles of dust stuck to my finger after I touched it. I guess it had not been touched in many years. On it was printed a quotation from Chairman Mao. "Policy and tactics constitute the life of the Party, to which leaders at all levels must pay full attention. Do not be negligent on any account."

As I opened it, I saw that the envelope contained nothing but the evaluation report upon her graduation from the Music School, her application for membership in the Communist Youth League, the application form of the graduating class, and the physical exam form of 1972, on which the doctor did not even record her pregnancy but only very professionally wrote, "The fundus of the uterus is positioned at 3–4 cm beneath the xiphisternum." The school authorities' graduation evaluation of her said, "She defied pressure and was among the earliest to rise in rebellion under the reign of terror by the reactionary capitalist roaders." There wasn't even a word about the punishment for her illegitimate pregnancy and her unauthorized trip to Guangzhou. In the envelope were also her confessions, her attacks against her family, and her denunciations of her mother for her suicide, but nothing negative from the school authorities. None. And yet, from 1973 to 1975, Yao Yao, left with no means of living, was in mortal fear of this brown-paper envelope locked up in a room, and cowered before those who mentioned it in threatening tones.

Zhang Xiaoxiao said, "Later, in about 1974, Yao Yao gave up all hopes of getting a job in Shanghai. She made up her mind to go abroad to be reunited with her father. I noticed her studying English. She had always been taking Russian classes at school, and only picked up English because she was determined to go abroad. She found a Linguaphone textbook printed before the Cultural Revolution. There was also a copy of the English version of *Quotations from Chairman Mao*. Yao Yao told me that she was going to risk everything this time. She said, 'Xiaoxiao, I'm at my wits' end. I'm going to put my life on the line this time.' I asked her how her plans were going to work out. The government would definitely not let a person with a disgraceful record like her go abroad.

To make things worse, she was going to the United States, something one wouldn't even dare whisper about. She said that (to get to Hong Kong) she had just one river to cross. She could take the bridge, or a boat, or she could swim across. She told me not to know too much, so as to stay safe. She said those were her mother's words to her—it's better not to know too much. I knew that having gone through so much, she was nervous about other people knowing what she was doing. So I gave her my word. That day, we indulged in reveries about the future. She said that over there, nobody knew what was contained in her dossier, that it was a place where her file would not follow her. I said yes, that would be great, so she could start her life all over again. She said she would go to school in America and really apply herself to her studies. Then she would be able to find a job. She wouldn't depend on her father but would stand on her own feet. I said yes. Over there, if she worked hard, she would be able to make something of herself. Then she said she would be a good person. I said that after the total change of scene, she would be rich. She could then come back to China, find her son, and take him away. What a nice family reunion that would be! At that point, with my own child still small, children were foremost in my thoughts about everything.

"I remember that Yao Yao's eyebrows flew up. Giving me a friendly slap, she said, 'Xiaoxiao, now you are talking!'"

Dengdeng said, "Towards the end of 1974, Kaikai was released from prison. They began to see each other again. I had the feeling that they were making some plan. Once when Sister and I stood talking on Auntie Shang's balcony, she told me that she had met Kaikai again. I said you'd better not see each other again. She fell silent. From that time on, she never brought up Kaikai again in our conversations, but I could sense that they were together again and often met somewhere outside."

Zhang Xiaoxiao said, "Yao Yao and Kaikai had no future at all if they didn't go abroad. After his release from prison, Kaikai was even more determined to go, so was Yao Yao. They often got together on the sly. I told Yao Yao to really watch out for herself this time. She said that, after having gone through so many terrible things, they were now just friends, not lovers anymore, and saw each other only to draw up plans to go abroad."

"She mentioned a bridge and something about swimming. Were they planning to steal across the border again? And she warned you against knowing anything about it," I said.

"They didn't say that straight out, so I couldn't have known, but Yao Yao did keep saying she was ready to put her life on the line.

"But then she panicked, because her communication with her father Yao Ke in America came to an abrupt end. Yao Ke was never heard from again. I learned only later that it was a problem with Yao Ke's mailbox. And Yao Ke thought Yao Yao had stopped writing. He dared not contact her, lest he bring her trouble. When visiting me, she would be so agitated that she couldn't even sit down and had to stand while talking with me. Sometimes, even talking was too much of an effort for her."

By that time, she was a thirty-year-old orphan with a lock of white hair hidden in her braid, and without a penny to her name.

Auntie Shang said, "Later, my husband, who was working in the Cultural Office of Zhejiang Province, pressed a man in position to help, who was also a relative of Yao Yao's, to find her a job. Through their intervention, Yao Yao finally got a job at the Song and Dance Ensemble of Zhejiang Province, and not a moment too soon, because the Conservatory had already issued Yao Yao an ultimatum. If she was not accepted anywhere within two months, they were going to take compulsory action and pack her off to Gansu or Qinghai, where someone like her would be acceptable. It was a good thing that Yao Yao finally found a position with the Song and Dance Ensemble of Zhejiang Province ahead of the deadline. My husband had housing in Hangzhou at the time, and we agreed that Yao Yao could live there and be taken care of. That took a load off my mind."

Everybody breathed easier for Yao Yao. At long last, life granted her a wish and showed her its first smile.

There was never a more pleasant parting of good friends. The last time Zhang Xiaoxiao saw Yao Yao, they reminisced about their childhood. Their favorite game had been to examine Shangguan Yunzhu's big wardrobe. They opened the door of the wardrobe and drew out her *qipao* one by one, admiring the graceful cut and the beautiful colors. They must have imagined themselves in them when they grew up.

In the dimly lit, bike-filled lobby of Wukang Building, Huang Zongjiang, who was there to see Sun Daolin, ran into Yao Yao. Cheerfully she said, "Uncle Huang! I am Yao Yao!" Huang Zongjiang saw a brilliant girlish smile. He said, "It was an innocent and bright smile, rarely seen in those days, especially in that dilapidated, dark lobby. It was like a ray of sun. I was deeply touched that she was still capable of such a smile. It was as if she had never been traumatized." So saying, he raised his eyebrows and his wrinkled face radiated with girlish affection, tenderness and joy. "Look! This was her smile. It never faded from my memory."

That year, Yao Yao turned 31. On her thirty-first birthday, she received a gift, a painting done by an artist friend of hers. It was a painting of red water lilies blooming on a bed of mud. They had a photograph taken together as a parting souvenir. That summer in Shanghai, revolutionary puritanism was already on its way out. The hairdressers on Huaihai Road began to blow their customers' hair into styles that they specified. But since perms were still not allowed, smart Shanghai women invented a technique using copper wire curlers. On the streets and in the parks, women cautiously but proudly showed off their unconventional hairdos. The temperature of the copper wire was hard to control. The curly hair-ends often showed signs of scorching. The black hair kinked up like instant noodles and turned brownish. When a gust of wind blew in their direction, the women would turn their heads and seek shelter from the wind, because the curls didn't stay in shape for very long. A gust of wind would easily blow their hair straight again.

Yao Yao heated up on the gas stove the kind of thick copper wire used in telephone lines, and wrapped her hair around the wire. After the copper wire cooled down, she took it off, leaving her hair curly, just like after a perm. This was how she did her hair for the photograph. Being as skillful as she was, she had not scorched her hair.

That year, thanks to efforts by Yao Yao and Cheng Shuyao, Dengdeng got transferred to Shanghai. Before Yao Yao was to leave for her job, she said to Dengdeng while cooking in Auntie Shang's kitchen,

"In the future, the two of us will have to 'hold on to each other for dear life,' as it were."

In the morning of September 23, 1975, in Shanghai, a drizzle heralded the advent of autumn. The next day, Yao Yao was to leave Shanghai and start her career. Her bags, all packed, were piled up in Auntie Shang's corridor. That morning, Yao Yao told Auntie Shang that she wanted to say goodbye to a friend and off she went on her bicycle.

That day, a delegation of Mexican athletes was scheduled to depart for Mexico from Shanghai. According to rules prevalent during the Cultural Revolution, a curfew was mandatory for streets that were to be used for the motorcades of foreign visitors. At 10:45 a.m. when Yao Yao was passing West Nanjing Road, which had already been closed to motor vehicles, a heavy truck from the Changjiang Shipping Company suddenly came into view on West Nanjing Road. A hook on the cabin door caught Yao Yao's plastic raincoat. Instantly she fell under the back wheels of the truck. Two solid and heavy black rubber wheels rolled over her chest and her head and flattened the upper part of her body against the pavement of West Nanjing Road.

An acquaintance of Cheng Shuyao's, riding in a bus passing on the Jiangning Road crossroads, saw pedestrians running along Jiangning Road to West Nanjing Road. "A fatal traffic accident!" they cried. From the bus window, which was streaky with rain, he saw a pool of blood grow on the wet pavement of West Nanjing Road like a gently expanding floating cloud. It was said that the upper part of Yao Yao's body had to be removed with iron spades from the street.

Someone took Kaikai to Zhang Xiaoxiao's home. No one knows how the news had reached him. He had gone to the mortuary of the crematorium to find Yao Yao's body, but it was not there. Her flattened body lay in the embalming suite. The Public Security Bureau asked Auntie Shang for a photo of Yao Yao so that the crematorium could reproduce Yao Yao's face with wax and make-up. Zhang Xiaoxiao said, "This happened when she was on her way to see a friend. I wonder which friend it was. Should that friend learn about this, imagine what a blow that would be to him or her!" Kaikai's face was suddenly drained of color.

Cheng Shuyao's old schoolmate Sun Daolin

and Shangguan Yunzhu's old friend Zhang Leping came to bid farewell to Yao Yao whom they knew from childhood, and were shocked at the sight of the wax face. It was one-fifth longer than the actual size. Dengdeng was preoccupied with identifying his sister and Cheng Shuyao didn't have the courage to see the body and shunned the funeral, so Zhang Xiaoxiao was the only one who distinctly heard the line from the memorial speech given by a representative of the Conservatory, "She was a person who never made any contribution to the country."

Zhang Xiaoxiao burst into tears.

In 1978, the Shanghai Film Bureau rehabilitated Shangguan Yunzhu and reversed the 1973 verdict that she "committed suicide not for fear of punishment but due to cancer as well as her misunderstanding of the revolution." The new verdict was "Shangguan Yunzhu was persecuted to death by followers of Lin Biao and the Gang of Four." A solemn memorial service was held in her honor.

That same year, because no one went to the Longhua Crematorium to claim back Yao Yao's ashes, which could be held there for three years only, the crematorium buried them deep in the ground as "ashes without a claimant."

In 1979, the Shanghai Conservatory of Music held a memorial service for all the professors and students who had been persecuted to death during the Cultural Revolution. The walls were covered with photographs of the departed. It was a ghastly sight, but Yao Yao's photo was not there, because she had died of a traffic accident, not of persecution.

That year, Dengdeng gave up his chances of getting a college education in Shanghai and with new resolve, went back to Beijing. He did not want to stay on in a city that had turned too bloody for him. He adopted Shangguan Yunzhu's real surname, Wei, and changed his name to Wei Ran, finally sharing the surname with his sister. If their names were juxtaposed, one could instantly tell that they were of the same family.

In 1995, Dengdeng who had finally settled down to a career as an editor, began to look for Yao Yao's son, his only clue being the child's birthday. With the help of a journalist from *Xinmin Evening News*, he located the child's adoptive father. Dengdeng had no intention of claiming the child back. He just wished to tell the story of Yao Yao's life to this child who had grown up in total ignorance of his birth mother's identity. Auntie Shang wanted to tell him that Yao Yao had wept under her quilt, feeling that she had done him an injustice. Cheng Yuxian kept at home all the letters that he had exchanged with Yao Yao from their first meeting to her death. He also had all the negatives of the photos, ready to hand them all over to Yao Yao's son some day, to let him know about his mother's life and have her belongings.

The child's adoptive parents didn't want to disrupt his peaceful life and to agitate him with things from the past. They didn't have the heart to tell him that he was in fact an orphan with a tragic family background. Impeccably polite but resolute, they said, "Please let him live his carefree life. We will tell him when he's older and more mature." That year, he was twenty-two. Many people in this narrative of ours supported their decision and hoped that his heart and mind would be protected against such pain.

In the afternoon of a wintry day five years later, Dengdeng and I sat at a table by the window in a coffee house on Middle Huaihai Road. Yao Yao's dorm was now part of the most expensive foreign furniture store in Shanghai. After Cheng Shuyao and Wu Yan passed away, their apartment was taken back by the government. Strangers moved in. The same thing had happened to Shangguan Yunzhu's apartment. The small apartment building still stood there. The Gothic-style windows still looked as if they had come out of a Jane Austen novel. With Shangguan Yunzhu, Cheng Shuyao, Yan Kai and Yao Ke all dead and gone, those who had close contact with Yao Yao dwindled in number. As for Kaikai, as soon as the country opened its door to the outside world, he went abroad to be reunited with his mother and severed all ties with Shanghai. Survivors were so tormented by memories of Yao Yao that they refused to mention her by way of warding off the torment, just like people in pain gnashing their teeth. They shunned the subject to let their wounds heal by themselves. It was only when the subject was brought up by someone else that they realized their memory of many details had faded, and that those events had affected their lives deeply, and now continued to disrupt their peaceful life. They didn't want to talk, in order to protect their hard-won peace of mind. In fact, the only one who, in spite of my constant interruptions, dived into his memories over and over again and put them in words, was Dengdeng, Yao Yao's flesh and blood. When he couldn't go on, he silently focused his eyes on one point on the floor until he could resume. But he never dodged my questions or gave perfunctory answers. I said, "Sorry, I made you feel sad." He replied, "It's okay. As long as you can write down a true historical record, that will be a commemoration in her honor. I still want to find my sister's son. I only have a vague idea that he's the co-owner of a business."

Not an unusual career for a young man in Shanghai. We watched pedestrians passing by. There were many young people, looking serious, calculating, far from downcast, and eager for action. Involuntarily, both of us kept our eyes out for young men of Yao Yao's son's age, 27 or 28, perhaps. They went past us, wearing English suits, American coats, Italian leather shoes, and Japanese-style trench coats. One of them might well have been Yao Yao's son. They walked past in haste, heading toward their future.

Stories by Contemporary Writers from Shanghai

The Little Restaurant
Wang Anyi

A Pair of Jade Frogs
Ye Xin

Forty Roses
Sun Yong

Goodby, Xu Hu!
Zhao Changtian

Vicissitudes of Life
Wang Xiaoying

The Elephant
Chen Cun

Folk Song
Li Xiao

The Messenger's Letter
Sun Ganlu

Ah, Blue Bird
Lu Xing'er

His One and Only
Wang Xiaoyu

When a Baby Is Born
Cheng Naishan

Dissipation
Tang Ying

Paradise on Earth
Zhu Lin

The Most Beautiful Face in the World
Xue Shu

Beautiful Days
Teng Xiaolan

Between Confidantes
Chen Danyan

She She
Zou Zou